THE
RAVEN
IN THE
FOREGATE

THE COMPLETE BROTHER CADFAEL SERIES

THE RAVEN IN THE FOREGATE

ELLIS PETERS

Book-of-the-Month Club
New York

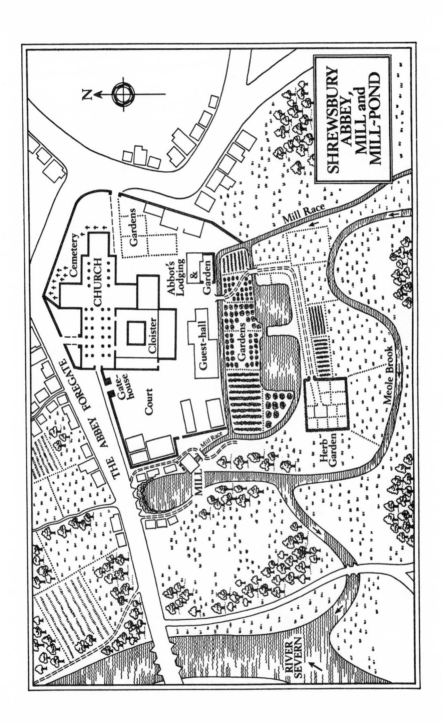

SHREWSBURY ABBEY, MILL and MILL-POND

N

Mill Race

Mill Race

Cemetery

CHURCH

Gardens

Cloister

Abbot's Lodging & Garden

Guest-hall

Gardens

Gate-house

Court

Meole Brook

THE ABBEY FOREGATE

MILL

Mill Race

Herb Garden

RIVER SEVERN

Chapter One

Abbot Radulfus came to chapter, on this first day of December, with a preoccupied and frowning face, and made short work of the various trivialities brought up by his obedientiaries. Though a man of few words himself, he was disposed, as a rule, to allow plenty of scope to those who were rambling and loquacious about their requests and suggestions, but on this day, plainly, he had more urgent matters on his mind.

'I must tell you,' he said, when he had swept the last trifle satisfactorily into its place, 'that I shall be leaving you for some days to the care of Father Prior, to whom, I expect and require, you shall be as obedient and helpful as you are to me. I am summoned to a council to be held at Westminster on the seventh day of this month, by the Holy Father's legate, Henry of Blois, bishop of Winchester. I shall return as soon as I can, but in my absence I desire you will make your prayers for a spirit of wisdom and reconciliation in this meeting of prelates, for the sake of the peace of this land.'

His voice was dry and calm to the point of resignation. For the past four years there had been precious little inclination to reconciliation in England between the warring rivals for the crown, and no very considerable wisdom shown on either side. But it was the business of the Church to continue to strive, and if possible to hope, even when the affairs of the land seemed to have reverted to the very same point where the civil war had begun, to repeat the whole unprofitable cycle all over again.

'I am well aware there are matters outstanding here,' said

the abbot, 'which equally require our attention, but they must wait for my return. In particular there is the question of a successor to Father Adam, lately vicar of this parish of Holy Cross, whose loss we are still lamenting. The advowson rests with this house. Father Adam has been for many years a much valued associate with us here in the worship of God and the cure of souls, and his replacement is a matter for both thought and prayer. Until my return, Father Prior will direct the parish services as he thinks fit, and all of you will be at his bidding.'

He swept one long, dark glance round the chapter house, accepted the general silence as understanding and consent, and rose.

'This chapter is concluded.'

'Well, at least if he leaves tomorrow he has good weather for the ride,' said Hugh Beringar, looking out from the open door of Brother Cadfael's workshop in the herb garden over grass still green, and a few surviving roses, grown tall and spindly by now but still budding bravely. December of this year of Our Lord 1141 had come in with soft-stepping care, gentle winds and lightly veiled skies, treading on tiptoe. 'Like all those shifting souls who turned to the Empress when she was in her glory,' said Hugh, grinning, 'and are now put to it to keep well out of sight while they turn again. There must be a good many holding their breath and making themselves small just now.'

'Bad luck for his reverence the papal legate,' said Cadfael, 'who cannot make himself small or go unregarded, whatever he does. His turning has to be done in broad daylight, with every eye on him. And twice in one year is too much to ask of any man.'

'Ah, but in the name of the Church, Cadfael, in the name of the Church! It's not the man who turns, it's the representative of Pope and Church, who must preserve the infallibility of both at all costs.'

Twice in one year, indeed, had Henry of Blois summoned

his bishops and abbots to a legatine council, once in Winchester on the seventh of April to justify his endorsement of the Empress Maud as ruler, when she was in the ascendant and had her rival King Stephen securely in prison in Bristol, and now at Westminster on the seventh of December to justify his swing back to Stephen, now that the King was free again, and the city of London had put a decisive end to Maud's bid to establish herself in the capital, and get her hands at last on the crown.

'If his head is not going round by now, it should be,' said Cadfael, shaking his own grizzled brown tonsure in mingled admiration and deprecation. 'How many spins does this make? First he swore allegiance to the lady, when her father died without a male heir, then he accepted his brother Stephen's seizure of power in her absence, thirdly, when Stephen's star is darkened he makes his peace – a peace of sorts, at any rate! – with the lady, and justifies it by saying that Stephen has flouted and aggrieved Holy Church. . . . Now must he turn the same argument about, and accuse the Empress, or has he something new in his scrip?'

'What is there new to be said?' asked Hugh, shrugging. 'No, he'll wring the last drop from his stewardship of Holy Church, and make the best of it that every soul there will have heard it all before, no longer ago than last April. And it will convince Stephen no more than it did Maud, but he'll let it pass with only a mild snarl or two, since he can no more afford to reject the backing of Henry of Blois than could Maud in her day. And the bishop will grit his teeth and stare his clerics in the eyes, and swallow his gall with a brazen face.'

'It may well be the last time he has to turn about-face,' said Cadfael, feeding his brazier with a few judiciously placed turves, to keep it burning with a slow and tempered heat. 'She has thrown away what's likely to be her only chance.'

A strange woman she had proved, King Henry's royal daughter. Married in childhood to the Holy Roman Emperor Henry V, she had so firmly ingratiated herself with her husband's people in Germany that when she was recalled to England, after his death, the populace had risen in consternation and grief to plead with her to stay. Yet here at home, when fate threw her enemy into her hands and held the crown suspended over her head, she had behaved with such vengeful arrogance, and exacted such penalties for past affronts, that the men of her capital city had risen just as indignantly, not to appeal to her to remain, but to drive her out and put a violent end to her hopes of ever becoming their ruler. And it was common knowledge that though she could turn even upon her own best allies with venom, yet she could also retain the love and loyalty of the best of the baronage. There was not a man of the first rank on Stephen's side to match the quality of her half-brother, Earl Robert of Gloucester, or her champion and reputed lover, Brian FitzCount, her easternmost paladin in his fortress at Wallingford. But it would take more than a couple of heroes to redeem her cause now. She had been forced to surrender her royal prisoner in exchange for her half-brother, without whom she could not hope to achieve anything. And here was England back to the beginning, with all to do again. For if she could not win, neither could she give up.

'From here where I stand now,' said Cadfael, pondering, 'these things seem strangely distant and unreal. If I had not been forty years in the world and among the armies myself, I doubt if I could believe in the times we live in but as a disturbed dream.'

'They are not so to Abbot Radulfus,' said Hugh with unwonted gravity. He turned his back upon the mild, moist prospect of the garden, sinking gently into its winter sleep, and sat down on the wooden bench against the timber wall. The small glow of the brazier, damped under the turf, burned on the bold, slender bones of his cheeks and jaw and brows, conjuring them out of deep shadows, and sparkling briefly in his black eyes before the lids and dark lashes quenched the sparks. 'That man would make a better adviser to kings than most that cluster round Stephen now he's free again. But he would not tell them what they want to hear, and they'd all stop their ears.'

'What's the news of King Stephen now? How has he borne this year of captivity? Is he likely to come out of it fighting, or has it dimmed his ardour? What is he likely to do next?'

'That I may be better able to answer after Christmas,' said Hugh. 'They say he's in good health. But she put him in chains, and that even he is not likely to forgive too readily. He's come out leaner and hungrier than he went in, and a gnaw in the belly may well serve to concentrate the mind. He was ever a man to begin a campaign or siege all fire the first day, weary of it if he got no gain by the third, and go off after another prey by the fifth. Maybe now he's learned to keep an unwavering eye fixed on one target until he fetches it down. Sometimes I wonder why we follow him, and never look round, then I see him roaring into personal battle as he did at Lincoln, and I know the reason well enough. Even when he has the woman as good as in his hands, as when she first landed at Arundel, and gives her an escort to her brother's fortress instead of having the good sense to seize her, I curse him for a fool, but I love him while I'm cursing him. What monumental folly of mistaken chivalry he'll commit next, only God knows. But I'll welcome the chance to see him again, and try to guess at his mind. For I'm bidden forth, Cadfael, like the abbot. King Stephen means to keep Christmas at Canterbury this year, and put on his crown again, for all to see which of two heads is the anointed monarch here. And he's called all his sheriffs to attend him and render account of their shires. Me among the rest, seeing we have here no properly appointed sheriff to render account.'

He looked up with a dark, sidelong smile into Cadfael's attentive and thoughtful face. 'A very sound move. He needs to know what measure of loyalty he has to rely on, after a year in prison, or close on a year. But there's no denying it may bring me a fall.'

For Cadfael it was a new and jolting thought. Hugh had

stepped into the office of sheriff perforce, when his superior, Gilbert Prestcote, had died of his battle wounds and the act of a desperate man, at a time when the King was already a prisoner in Bristol castle, with no power to appoint or to demote any officer in any shire. And Hugh had served him and maintained his peace here without authority, and deserved well of him. But now that he was free to make and break again, would Stephen confirm so young and so minor a nobleman in office, or use the appointment to flatter and bind to himself some baron of the march?

'Folly!' said Cadfael firmly. 'The man is a fool only towards himself. He made you deputy to his man out of nowhere, when he saw your mettle. What does Aline say of it?'

Hugh could not hear his wife's name spoken without a wild, warm softening of his sharp, subtle face, nor could Cadfael speak it without relaxing every solemnity into a smile. He had witnessed their courtship and their marriage, and was godfather to their son, two years old this coming Christmastide. Aline's girlish, flaxen gentleness had grown into a golden, matronly calm to which they both turned in every need.

'Aline says that she has no great confidence in the gratitude of princes, but that Stephen has the right to choose his own officers, wisely or foolishly.'

'And you?' said Cadfael.

'Why, if he gives me his countenance and writ I'll go on keeping all his borders for him, and if not, then I'll go back to Maesbury and keep the north, at least, against Chester, if the earl tries again to enlarge his palatinate. And Stephen's man must take charge of west, east and south. And you, old friend, must pay a visit or two over Christmas, while I'm away, and keep Aline company.'

'Of all of us,' said Cadfael piously, 'that makes me the best blessed at this coming feast. I'll pray good joy to my abbot in his mission, and to you in yours. My joy is assured.'

*   *   *

They had buried old Father Adam, seventeen years vicar of the parish of Holy Cross in the Foregate of Shrewsbury, only one week before Abbot Radulfus was summoned to the legatine council at Westminster. The advowson of the living was vested in the abbey, and the great church of Saint Peter and Saint Paul was equally the parish church of Holy Cross, the nave open to the people living here outside the town gates, in this growing suburb which almost considered itself a borough like the borough within the walls. The reeve of the Foregate, Erwald the wheelwright, publicly if unofficially used the title of provost, and abbey, church and town humoured his harmless flourish, for the Monks' Foregate was a relatively law-abiding, respectable district, and gave barely any trouble to the properly constituted authorities of the town itself. An occasional squabble between seculars and abbey, a brief tangle between the high-spirited young of Foregate and town, what was there in that to worry anyone beyond the day?

Father Adam had been there so long that all the young had grown up under his easy-going shadow, and all the old had known him as one of themselves, hardly set apart by his office. He had lived alone in his little house up a narrow alley opposite the church, looking after himself, with only an elderly freeman to take care of his glebe and his strip fields in the country part of the parish, for Holy Cross spread wide outside the main street of the Foregate. A big parish, a population made up equally of the craftsmen and merchants of the suburb and the cottars and villagers in the countryside. It was a matter of importance to them all what manner of priest they got in succession to Father Adam. The old man himself, from whatever gentle purgatory now contained him, would be keeping an anxious eye on his own.

Abbot Radulfus had presided at Adam's funeral, and Prior Robert at his most dignified and elegiac, tall and silvery and consciously patrician, had pronounced his eulogy, perhaps with a slight touch of condescension, for Adam had been barely literate, and a man of humble origins and no pretentions. But it was Cynric, the verger of Holy Cross, who had been with the priest through most of his years of office, who had best spoken his epitaph, and that privately, over the trimming of the candles on the parish altar, to Brother Cadfael, who had halted in passing through to say a word of personal sympathy to the man who would surely miss the dead most deeply.

'A sad, kind man,' said Cynric, his deep-sunk eyes narrowed on the wick he was trimming, and his low voice as grainy and grudging as ever, 'a tired man, with a soft spot for sinners.'

It was rare enough for Cynric to utter thirteen words together, except by way of the responses learned by heart in the holy office. Thirteen words of his own had the force of prophecy. A sad man, because he had been listening to and bearing with the perpetual failures of humankind for seventeen years, a tired man because endless consoling and chiding and forgiving takes it out of any man by the time he's sixty, especially one with neither malice nor anger in his own make-up. A kind man, because he had somehow managed to preserve compassion and hope even against the tide of human fallibility. Yes, Cynric had known him better than anyone. He had absorbed, in the years of his service, something of the same qualities without the authority.

'You'll feel the want of him,' said Cadfael. 'So shall we all.'

'He'll not be far,' said Cynric, and snipped the dead wick with thumb and finger.

The verger was a man past fifty, but there was no knowing by how many years, for he himself did not know the exact year of his birth, though he knew the day and month. He was dark of hair and eyes, and sallow-skinned, and went in a rusty black gown somewhat frayed at the hems from long years of wear, and he lived in the tiny upper room over the north porch where Father Adam robed and kept his church furnishings. A taciturn, grave, durable man, built upon long, strong bones, but very meagre in flesh, as much by reason of the hermit's forgetfulness as any want of means. He came of

14

a country family of free folk, and had a brother somewhere north of the town with a grown family, and very occasionally at feast or holiday he visited there, but that happened very rarely now, his whole life being centred here in the great church and the small upper room. So spare, silent and dark a form and face might have aroused awe and avoidance, but did not, since what the darkness and the silence covered was known to all, even the mischievous boys of the Foregate, and inspired no fear or revulsion at all. A good man, with his own preferences and peculiarities, and certainly no talker, but if you needed him, he was there, and like his master, would not send you away empty.

Those who could not be easy with his mute company at least respected him, and those who could included the most innocent and guileless. Children and dogs would sit companionably on the steps of the north porch with him in summer weather, and do all the talking necessary to such a friendship, after their own fashion, while he listened. Many a mother in the Foregate, content to see her young consorting so familiarly with a respectable churchman, had wondered why Cynric had never married and had children of his own, since plainly he had an affinity for them. It could not be because of his office of verger, for there were still plenty of married priests scattered through the parishes of the shire, and no one thought any wrong of them. The new order of clerics without women was only just beginning to make headway here, no one, not even bishops, had yet begun to look sidewise at those of the old school who did not conform. Monks were monks, and had made their choice, but surely the secular clergy could still be secular without reproach.

'He had no living kin?' asked Cadfael. For of all men remaining behind, Cynric would know.

'None.'

'He was newly priest here,' said Cadfael, 'when I came first from Woodstock with Abbot Heribert – Prior Heribert he was then, for Abbot Godefrid was still alive. You came, as I

15

remember, a year or two later. You're a younger man than I. You and I between us could put together a history of cowl and cassock here in the Foregate all this long while. It would make a very handsome memorial to Father Adam. No falling out, no falling off. He had his everlasting penitents, but that was his glory, that they always came back. They could not do without him. And he kept his thread that drew them back, whether they would or no.'

'So he did,' said Cynric, and clipped the last blackened wick with a snap of his finger-nails, and straightened the candlesticks on the parish altar, standing back a pace with narrowed lids to check that they stood correct as soldiers on guard.

His throat creaked, forcing unwilling chords to flex, when he used more words. The strings protested now. 'Is there a man in mind?'

'No,' said Cadfael, 'or Father Abbot would have told you. He goes south by forced rides tomorrow to the legate's council in Westminster, and this presentation must wait his return, but he's promised haste. He knows the need. You may well get Brother Jerome now and again until the abbot returns, but never doubt that Radulfus has the parish very much at heart.'

To that Cynric nodded silent assent, for the relations between cloister and parish here had been harmonious under three abbots in succession, all the years of Father Adam's incumbency, whereas in some churches thus shared, as everyone knew, there was constant friction, the monastics grudging the commonalty room in their enclave and entry to their privileged buildings, and the secular priest putting up a fight for his rights to avoid being elbowed out. Not so here. Perhaps it was the modest goodness of Father Adam that had done the lion's share in keeping the peace, and making the relationship easy.

'He liked a sup now and again,' said Cadfael meditatively. 'I still have some of a wine he liked – distilled with herbs, good for the blood and heart. Come and take a cup with me in the garden, some afternoon, Cynric, and we'll drink to him.'

'I will so,' said Cynric, and relaxed for one moment into his rare, indulgent smile, the same by which children and dogs found him out and approached him with confidence.

They crossed the chill tiles of the nave together, and Cynric went out by the north porch, and up to his little dark room above. Cadfael looked after him until the door had closed between. All these years they had been within arm's reach of each other, and on the best of terms, yet never familiar. Who had ever been familiar with Cynric? Since the ties with his mother loosened, and he turned his back on home, whatever and wherever that home had been, perhaps only Father Adam had truly drawn near to him. Two solitaries together make a very special matched pair, two in one. Yes, of all the mourners for Father Adam, and they must be many, Cynric must now be the most painfully bereaved.

They had lighted the fire in the warming room for the first time when December came in, and in the relaxed half-hour between Collations and Compline, when tongues were allowed considerable licence, there was far more talk and speculation about the parish cure than about the legate's council in Westminster, to which Abbot Radulfus had just set out. Prior Robert had withdrawn into the abbot's lodging, as representing that dignitary in his absence, which gave further freedom to the talkative, but his chaplain and shadow, Brother Jerome, in his turn took upon himself the duty and privilege of representing the prior, and Brother Richard, the sub-prior, was too easy-going, not to say indolent, to assert himself with any vigour.

A meagre man in the flesh was Brother Jerome, but he made up for it in zeal, though there were those who found that zeal too narrowly channelled, and somewhat dehydrated of the milk of human tolerance. Which rendered it understandable that he should consider Father Adam to have been rather over-supplied with that commodity.

'Certainly a man of virtue himself,' said Jerome, 'I would not for a moment take that from him, we all know he served devotedly. But somewhat loose upon others who did offend. His discipline was too slack, and his penances too light and too indulgently given. Who spares the sinner condones the sin.'

'There's been good order and neighbourliness in his parish the length of his life here,' said Brother Ambrose the almoner, whose office brought him into contact with the poorest of the poor throughout the Foregate. 'I know how they speak of him. He left a cure ready and fit for another to step into, with the general goodwill open to whoever comes, because the general goodwill was there to speed the one departed.'

'Children will always be glad of a weak master who never uses the rod,' said Jerome sagely, 'and rascals of a judge who lets them off lightly. But the payment that falls due later will be fearful. Better they should be brought up harshly against the wages of sin now, and lay up safety for their souls hereafter.'

Brother Paul, master of the novices and the boys, who very rarely laid a hand upon his pupils, and certainly only when they had well deserved it, smiled and held his peace.

'In too much mercy is too little kindness,' pronounced Jerome, conscious of his own eloquence, and mindful of his reputation as a preacher. 'The Rule itself decrees that where the child offends he must be beaten, and these folk of the Foregate, what are they but children?'

They were called by the bell to Compline at that moment, but in any case it was unlikely that any of them would have troubled to argue with Jerome, whose much noise and small effect hardly challenged notice. No doubt he would preach stern sermons at the parish Mass, on the two days allotted to him, but there would be very few of the regular attenders there to listen to him, and even those who did attend would let his homily in at one ear and out at the other, knowing his office here could last but a few days.

For all that, Cadfael went to his bed that night very thoughtful, and though he heard a few whispered exchanges in the dortoir, himself kept silence, mindful of the rule that the words of Compline, the completion, the perfecting of the day's worship, should be the last words uttered before sleep, that the mind should not be distracted from the *'Opus Dei'*. Nor was it. For the words lingered with him between sleep and waking, the same words over and over, faintly returning. By chance the psalm was the sixth. He took it with him into slumber.

'Domine, ne in furore – O Lord, rebuke me not in thine anger, neither chasten me in thy displeasure. . . . Have mercy upon me, O Lord, for I am weak. . . .'

Chapter Two

On the tenth day of December, Abbot Radulfus returned, riding in at the gatehouse just as the daylight was fading, and the brethren were within at Vespers. Thus the porter was the only witness of his arrival, and of the embellished entourage he brought back with him, and not until the next day at chapter did the brothers hear all that he had to tell, or as much of it as concerned the abbey itself. But Brother Porter, the soul of discretion when required, could also be the best-informed gossip in the enclave to his special friends, and Cadfael learned something of what was toward that same night, in one of the carrels in the cloister, immediately after Vespers.

'He's brought back with him a priest, a fine tall fellow – not above thirty-five years or so I'd guess him to be. He's bedded now in the guest hall, they rode hard today to get home before dark. Not a word has Father Abbot said to me, beyond giving me my orders to let Brother Denis know he has a guest for the night, and to take care of the other two. For there's a woman come with the priest, a decent soul going grey and very modestly conducted, that I take to be some sort of aunt or housekeeper to the priest, for I was bidden get one of the lay grooms to show her the way to Father Adam's cottage, and that I did. And not the woman alone, there's another young servant lad with her, that waits on the pair of them and does their errands. A widow and her son they could be, in the priest's service. Off he goes with only Brother Vitalis, as always, and comes back with three more, and two extra horses. The young lad brought the woman pillion behind him. And what do you make of all that?'

'Why, there's but one way of it,' said Cadfael, after giving the matter serious thought. 'The lord abbot has brought back a priest for Holy Cross from the southlands, and his household with him. The man himself is made comfortable in the guest hall overnight, while his domestics go to open up the empty house and get a good fire going for him, and food in store, and the place warmed and ready. And tomorrow at chapter, no doubt, we shall hear how the abbot came by him, and which of all the bishops gathered there recommended him to the benefice.'

'It's what I myself was thinking,' agreed the porter, 'though it would have been more to the general mind, I fancy, if a local man had been advanced to the vacancy. Still, it's what a man is that counts, not his name nor where he came from. No doubt the lord abbot knows his business best.' And he went off briskly, probably to whisper the news into one or two other discreet ears before Compline. Certainly several of the brothers came to the next morning's chapter already forewarned and expectant, alertly waiting for the new man to be first heralded, and then produced for inspection. For though it was very unlikely that anyone would raise objections to a man chosen by Abbot Radulfus, yet the whole chapter had rights in the presentation to the living, and Radulfus was not the man to infringe its privileges.

'I have made all possible haste to return to you,' the abbot began, when the normal routine matters had been quickly dealt with. 'In brief, I must report to you of the legatine council held at Westminster, that the discussions and decisions there have brought the Church back into full allegiance to King Stephen. The King himself was present to confirm the establishment of this relationship, and the legate to declare him blessed by the countenance of the Apostolic See, and the followers of the Empress, if they remain recalcitrant, as enemies of King and Church. There is no need,' said the abbot, somewhat drily, 'to go into further detail here.'

None, thought Cadfael, attentive in his chosen stall, conveniently sheltered behind a pillar in case he nodded off when material matters became tiresome. No need for us to hear the spiral manipulations by which the legate extricated himself from all his difficulties. But beyond doubt, Hugh would get a full account of all.

'What does more nearly concern this house,' said Radulfus, 'is certain conference I had with Bishop Henry of Winchester in private. Knowing of the cure left vacant here at Holy Cross, he recommended to me a priest of his own following, at present waiting for a benefice. I have talked with the man in question, and found him in every way able, scholarly and fitted for advancement. His personal life is austere and simple, his scholarship I have myself tested.'

It was a point powerful enough, by contrast with Father Adam's want of learning, though it would count for more with the brothers here than with the folk of the Foregate.

'Father Ailnoth is thirty-six years of age,' said the abbot, 'and comes rather late to a parish by reason of having served as a clerk to Bishop Henry, loyally and efficiently, for four years, and the bishop desires to reward his diligence now by seeing him settled in a cure. For my part, I am satisfied that he is both suitable and deserving. But if you will bear with me so far, brothers, I will have him called in to give account of himself, and answer whatever you may wish to ask him.'

A stir of interest, consent and curiosity went round the chapter house, and Prior Robert, surveying the heads nodding in anticipation and obeying the abbot's glance, went out to summon the candidate.

Ailnoth, thought Cadfael, a Saxon name, and reported as a fine, tall fellow. Well, better than some Norman hanger-on from the fringes of the court. And he formed a mental picture of a big young man with fresh, ruddy skin and fair hair, but dismissed it in a breath when Father Ailnoth came in on Prior Robert's heels, and took his stand with composed grace in the middle of the chapter house, where he could be seen by all.

He was indeed a fine, tall fellow, wide-shouldered, muscular, fluent and rapid in gait, erect and very still when he had taken his stand. And a very comely man, too, in his own fashion, but so far from Saxon pallor that he was blacker of hair and eye than Hugh Beringar himself. He had a long, patrician countenance, olive-skinned and with no warmer flush of red in his well-shaven cheeks. The black hair that ringed his tonsure was straight as wire, and thick, and clipped with such precision that it looked almost as if it had been applied with black paint. He made an austere obeisance to the abbot, folded his hands, which were large and powerful, at the waist of his black gown, and waited to be catechised.

'I present to this assembly Father Ailnoth,' said Radulfus, 'whom I propose we should prefer to the cure of Holy Cross. Examine him of his own wishes in this matter, his attainments and his past service, and he will answer freely.'

And freely indeed he did answer, launched by a first gracious word of welcome from Prior Robert, who clearly found his appearance pleasing. He answered questions briefly and fluently, like one who never has had and never expects to have any lack of confidence or any time to waste, and his voice, pitched a shade higher than Cadfael had expected from so big a man and so broad a chest, rang with an assured authority. He accounted for himself forcefully, declared his intent to pursue his duty with energy and integrity, and awaited the verdict upon himself with steely confidence. He had excellent Latin, some Greek, and was versed in accountancy, which promised well for his church management. His acceptance was assured.

'If I may make one request, Father Abbot,' he said finally, 'I should be greatly thankful if you could find some work here among your lay servants for the young man who has travelled here with me. He is the nephew and only kin of my housekeeper, the widow Hammet, and she entreated me to let him come here with her and find some employment locally. He is landless and without fortune. My lord abbot, you have seen that he is healthy and sturdy and not afraid of hard work, and he has been willing and serviceable to us all on the journey. He has, I believe, some inclination to the cloistered life, though as yet he is undecided. If you could give him work for a while it might settle his mind.'

'Ah, yes, the young man Benet,' said the abbot. 'He seems a well-conditioned youth, I agree. Certainly he may come, upon probation, no doubt work can be found for him. There must be a deal of things to be done about the grange court, or in the gardens. . . .'

'Indeed there is, Father,' Cadfael spoke up heartily. 'I could make good use of a younger pair of hands, there's much of the rough digging for the winter still to be done, some of the ground in the kitchen garden has only now been cleared. And the pruning in the orchard – heavy work. With the winter coming on, short days, and Brother Oswin gone to Saint Giles, to the hospice, I shall be needing a helper. I should shortly have been asking for another brother to come and work with me, as is usual, though through the summer I've managed well enough.'

'True! And some of the ploughing in the Gaye remains to be done, and around Christmas, or soon after, the lambing will begin in the hill granges, if the young man is no longer needed here. Yes, by all means send Benet to us. Should he later find other employment more to his advantage, he may take it with our goodwill. In the meantime hard labour here for us will do him no harm.'

'I will tell him so,' said Ailnoth, 'and he will be as thankful to you as I am. His aunt would have been sad at leaving him behind, seeing he is the only younger kinsman she has, to be helpful to her. Shall I send him here today?'

'Do so, and tell him he may ask at the gatehouse for Brother Cadfael. Leave us now to confer, Father,' said the abbot, 'but wait in the cloister, and Father Prior will bring you word of our decision.'

Ailnoth bowed his head with measured reverence, withdrew a respectful pace or two backwards from the abbot's presence, and strode out of the chapter house, his black, handsome head erect and confident. His gown swung like half-spread wings to the vigour of his stride. He was already sure, as was everyone present, that the cure of Holy Cross was his.

'It went much as you have probably supposed,' said Abbot Radulfus, somewhat later in the day, in the parlour of his own lodging, with a modest fire burning on the chimney stone, and Hugh Beringar seated opposite him across the glow. The abbot's face was still a little drawn and grey with tiredness, his deep-set eyes a little hollow. The two knew each other very well by this time, and had grown accustomed to sharing with complete confidence, for the sake of order and England, whatever they gathered of events and tendencies, without ever questioning whether they shared the same opinions. Their disciplines were separate and very different, but their acceptance of service was one, and mutually recognised.

'The bishop had little choice,' said Hugh simply. 'Virtually none, now the King is again free, and the Empress again driven into the west, with little foothold in the rest of England. I would not have wished myself in his shoes, nor do I know how I would have handled his difficulties. Let him who is certain of his own valour cast blame, I cannot.'

'Nor I. But for all that can be said, the spectacle is not edifying. There are, after all, some who have never wavered, whether fortune favoured or flayed them. But it is truth that the legate had received the Pope's letter, which he read out to us in conference, reproving him for not enforcing the release of the King, and urging him to insist upon it above all else. And who dare wonder if he made the most of it? And besides, the King came there himself. He entered the hall and made formal complaint against all those who had sworn fealty to him, and then suffered him to lie in prison, and come near to slaying him.'

'But then sat back and let his brother use his eloquence to

worm his way out of the reproach,' said Hugh, and smiled. 'He has the advantage of his cousin and rival, he knows when to mellow and forget. She neither forgets nor forgives.'

'Well, true. But it was not a happy thing to hear. Bishop Henry made his defence, frankly owning he had had no choice open to him but to accept the fortune as it fell, and receive the Empress. He said he had done what seemed the best and only thing, but that she had broken all her pledges, outraged all her subjects, and made war against his own life. And to conclude, he pledged the Church again to King Stephen, and urged all men of consequence and goodwill to serve him. He took some credit,' said Abbot Radulfus with sad deliberation, 'for the liberation of the King to himself. And outlawed from the Church all those who continued to oppose him.'

'And mentioned the Empress, or so I've heard,' said Hugh equally drily, 'as the countess of Anjou.' It was a title the Empress detested, as belittling both her birth and her rank by her first marriage, a king's daughter and the widow of an emperor, now reduced to a title borrowed from her none-too-loved and none-too-loving second husband, Geoffrey of Anjou, her inferior in every particular but talent, common sense and efficiency. All he had ever done for Maud was give her a son. Of the love she bore to the boy Henry there was no doubt at all.

'No one raised a voice against what was said,' the abbot mentioned almost absently. 'Except an envoy from the lady, who fared no better than the one who spoke, last time, for King Stephen's queen. Though this one, at least, was not set upon by assassins in the street.'*

Inevitably those two legatine councils, one in April, one in December, had been exact and chilling mirror-images, fortune turning her face now to one faction, now to the other, and taking back with the left hand what she had given with the right. There might yet be as many further reversals

*The Pilgrim of Hate.

before ever there was an end in sight.

'We are back where we began,' said the abbot, 'and nothing to show for months of misery. And what will the King do now?'

'That I shall hope to find out during the Christmas feast,' said Hugh, rising to take his leave. 'For I'm summoned to my lord, Father, like you. King Stephen wants all his sheriffs about him at his court at Canterbury, where he keeps the feast, to render account of our stewardships. Me among them, as his sheriff here for want of a better. What he'll do with his freedom remains to be seen. They say he's in good health and resolute spirits, if that means anything. As for what he means to do with me – well, that, no doubt, I shall discover, in due time.'

'My son, I trust he'll have the good sense to leave well alone. For here,' said Radulfus, 'we have at least preserved what good we can, and by the present measure in this unhappy realm, it *is* well with this shire. But I doubt whatever he does else can only mean more fighting and more wretchedness for England. And you and I can do nothing to prevent or better it.'

'Well, if we cannot give England peace,' said Hugh, smiling somewhat wryly, 'at least let's see what you and I can do between us for Shrewsbury.'

After dinner in the refectory Brother Cadfael made his way across the great court, rounded the thick, dark mass of the box hedge – grown straggly now, he noted, and ripe for a final clipping before growth ceased in the cold – and entered the moist flower gardens, where leggy roses balanced at a man's height on their thin, leafless stems, and still glowed with invincible light and life. Beyond lay his herb garden, walled and silent, all its small, square beds already falling asleep, naked spears of mint left standing stiff as wire, cushions of thyme flattened to the ground, crouching to protect their remaining leaves, yet over all a faint surviving fragrance of the summer's spices. Partly a memory, perhaps, partly drifting out from the open door of his workshop, where bunches of dried herbs swung from the eaves and the beams within, but surely, also, still emanating from these drowsy minor manifestations of God, grown old and tired now only to grow young and vigorous again with the spring. Green phoenixes every one, visible proof, if any were needed, of perpetual life.

Within the wall it was mild and still, a sanctuary within a sanctuary. Cadfael sat down on the bench in his workshop, facing the open door, and composed himself at ease to employ his half-hour of permitted repose in meditation rather than sleep. The morning had provided plenty of food for thought, and he did his best thinking alone here in his own small kingdom.

So that, he thought, is the new priest of Holy Cross. Now why did Bishop Henry take the trouble to bestow on us one of his own household clerks, and one he valued, at that? One who either was born with or has acquired by reverent imitation what I take to be his overlord's notable qualities? Is it possible that two masterful, confident, proud men had become one too many for comfort, and Henry was glad to part with him? Or is the legate, after the humiliation of publicly eating his own words twice in one year, and the damage that may well have done to his prestige – after all that, has he been taking this opportunity of courting all his bishops and abbots by taking a fatherly interest in all their wants and needs? Flattering them by his attentions to prop up what might be stumbling allegiance? That is also possible, and he might be willing to sacrifice even a valued clerk to feel certain of a man like Radulfus. But one thing is sure, Cadfael concluded firmly, our abbot would not have been a party to such an appointment if he had not been convinced he was getting a man fit for the work.

He had closed his eyes, to think the better, and braced his back comfortably against the timber wall, sandalled feet crossed before him, hands folded in the sleeves of his habit, so still that to the young man approaching along the gravel path he seemed asleep. Others, unused to such complete stillness in a waking man, had sometimes made that mistake with Brother Cadfael. Cadfael heard the footsteps, wary and soft as they were. Not a brother, and the lay servants were few in number, and seldom had occasion to come here. Nor would they approach so cautiously if they had some errand here. Not sandals, these, but old, well-worn shoes, and their wearer imagined they trod silently, and indeed they came close to it, if Cadfael had not had the hearing of a wild creature. Outside the open door the steps halted, and for a long moment the silence became complete. He studies me, thought Cadfael. Well, I know what he sees, if I don't know what he makes of it: a man past sixty, in robust health, bar the occasional stiffness in the joints proper to his age, squarely made, blunt-featured, with wiry brown hair laced with grey, and in need of a trim, come to think of it! – round a shaven crown that's been out in all weathers for many a year. He weighs me, he measures me, and takes his time about it.

He opened his eyes. 'I may look like a mastiff,' he said amiably, 'but it's years now since I bit anyone. Step in, and never hesitate.'

So brisk and unexpected a greeting, so far from drawing the visitor within, caused him to take a startled pace backwards, so that he stood full in the soft noon light of the day, to be seen clearly. A young fellow surely not above twenty, of the middle height but very well put together, dressed in wrinkled cloth hose of an indeterminate drab colour, scuffed leather shoes very down at heel, a dark brown cotte rubbed slightly paler where the sleeves chafed the flanks, and belted with a frayed rope girdle, and a short, caped capuchon thrown back on his shoulders. The coarse linen of his shirt showed at the neck, unlaced, and the sleeves of the cotte were short on him, showing a length of paler wrist above good brown hands. A compact, stout pillar of young manhood stood sturdily to be appraised, and once the immediate check had passed, even a long and silent appraisal seemed to reassure him rather than to make him uneasy, for a distinct spark lit in his eye, and an irrepressible grin hovered about his mouth as he said very respectfully:

'They told me at the gatehouse to come here. I'm looking for a brother named Cadfael.'

He had a pleasant voice, pitched agreeably low but with a fine, blithe ring to it, and just now practising a meekness which did not seem altogether at home on his tongue. Cadfael continued to study him with quickening interest. A mop of shaggy light-brown curls capped a shapely head poised on an elegant neck, and the face that took such pains to play the rustic innocent abashed before his betters was youthfully rounded of cheek and chin, but very adequately supplied with bone, too, and shaven clean as the schoolboy it aimed at presenting. A guileless face, but for the suppressed smoulder of mischief in the wide hazel eyes, changeable and fluid like peat water flowing over sunlit pebbles of delectable, autumnal greens and browns. There was nothing he could do about that merry sparkle. Asleep, the angelic simpleton might achieve conviction, but not with those eyes open.

'Then you have found him,' said Cadfael. 'That name belongs to me. And you, I take it, must be the young fellow who came here with the priest, and wants work with us for a while.' He rose, gathering himself without haste. Their eyes came virtually on a level. Dancing, brook-water eyes the boy had, scintillating with winter sunlight. 'What was the name they gave you, son?'

'N . . . name?' The stammer was a surprise, and the sudden nervous flickering of long brown lashes that briefly veiled the lively eyes was the first sign of unease Cadfael had detected in him. 'Benet – my name's Benet. My Aunt Diota is widow to a decent man, John Hammet, who was a groom in the lord bishop's service, so when he died Bishop Henry found a place for her with Father Ailnoth. That's how we came here. They're used to each other now for three years and more. And I begged to come here along with them to see could I find work near to her. I'm not skilled, but what I don't know I can learn.'

Very voluble now, all at once, and no more stammering, either, and he had stepped within, into shadow from the midday light, quenching somewhat of his perilous brightness. 'He said you could make use of me here,' said the vibrant voice, meekly muted. 'Tell me what to do, and I'll do it.'

'And a very proper attitude to work,' allowed Cadfael. 'You'll be sharing the life here within the enclave, so I'm told. Where have they lodged you? Among the lay servants?'

'Nowhere yet,' said the boy, his voice cautiously recovering its spring and resonance. 'But I'm promised a bed here within. I'd just as soon be out of the priest's house. There's a parish fellow looks after his glebe, they tell me, so there's no need for me there.'

'Well, there's need enough here,' said Cadfael heartily, 'for what with one thing and another I'm behind with the rough digging that ought to be done before the frosts come, and I've half a dozen fruit trees here in the small orchard that need pruning about Christmas time. Brother Bernard will be wanting to borrow you to help with the ploughing in the Gaye, where our main gardens are – you'll scarcely be familiar with the lie of the land yet, but you'll soon get used to it. I'll see you're not snatched away until I've had the worth of you here. Come, then, and see what we have for you within the walls.'

Benet had come a few paces more into the hut, and was looking about him with curiosity and mild awe at the array of bottles, jars and flagons that furnished Brother Cadfael's shelves, the rustling bunches of herbs that sighed overhead in the faint stirrings of air from the open door, the small brass scales, the three mortars, the single gently bubbling wine-jar, the little wooden bowls of medicinal roots, and a batch of small white lozenges drying on a marble slab. His round-eyed, open-mouthed stare spoke for him. Cadfael half-expected him to cross himself defensively against such ominous mysteries, but Benet stopped short of that. Just as well, thought Cadfael, alerted and amused, for I should not quite have believed in it.

'This, too, you can learn, if you put your mind to it diligently enough,' he said drily, 'but it will take you some years. Mere medicines – God made every ingredient that goes into them, there's no other magic. But let's begin with what's needed most. There's a good acre of vegetable garden beds to rough-dig, and a small mountain of well-weathered stable muck to cart and spread on the main butts and the rose beds. And the sooner we get down to it, the sooner it will be done. Come and see!'

The boy followed him willingly enough, his light, lively eyes scanning everything with interest. Beyond the fish ponds, in the two pease fields that ran down the slope to the Meole Brook, the western boundary of the enclave, the haulms had long since been cut close and dried for stable bedding, and the roots ploughed back into the soil, but there would be a heavy and dirty job there spreading much of the ripened and tempered manure from the stable yard and the byres. There were the few fruit trees in the small orchard to be pruned, but such growth as remained in the grass, in this mild opening of the month, was cropped neatly by two yearling lambs. The flower beds wore their usual somewhat ragged autumn look, but would do with one last weeding, if time served, before all growth ceased in the cold. The kitchen garden, cleared of its crops, lay weedy and trampled, waiting for the spade, a dauntingly large expanse. But it seemed that nothing could daunt Benet.

'A goodish stretch,' he said cheerfully, eyeing the long main butt with no sign of discouragement. 'Where will I find the tools?'

Cadfael showed him the low shed where they were to be found, and was interested to note that the young man looked round him among the assembly with a slightly doubtful face, though he soon selected the iron-shod wooden spade appropriate to the job in hand, and even viewed the length of the ground ahead and started his first row with judgement and energy, if not with very much skill.

'Wait!' said Cadfael, noting the thin, worn shoes the boy wore. 'If you thrust like that in such wear you'll have a swollen foot before long. I have wooden pattens in my hut that you can strap under your feet and shove as hard as you please. But no need to rush at it, or you'll be in a muck sweat before you've done a dozen rows. What you must do is set an even pace, get a rhythm into it, and you can go on all day, the spade will keep time for you. Sing to it if you have breath enough, or hum with it and save your breath. You'll be surprised how the rows will multiply.' He caught himself up there, somewhat belatedly aware that he was giving away too much of what he had already observed. 'Your work's been mainly with horses, as I heard,' he said blandly. 'There's an art in every labour.' And he went to fetch the wooden pattens he had himself carved out to shoe his own feet against either harsh digging or deep mire, before Benet could bridle in self-defence.

Thus shod and advised, Benet began very circumspectly, and Cadfael stayed only to see him launched into a good, steady action before he took himself off into his workshop, to be about his ordinary business of pounding up green herbs for an ointment of his own concoction, good against the chapped hands that would surely make their usual January appearance among the copyists and illuminators in the scriptorium. There would be coughs and colds, too, no doubt, later on, and now was the right time to prepare such of his medicines as would keep through the winter.

When it was almost time to clear away his impedimenta and prepare for Vespers he went out to see how his acolyte was faring. No one likes to be watched at his work, especially if he comes raw to the practice, and maybe a thought sensitive about his lack of skill and experience. Cadfael was impressed by the great surge the young man had made down the formidable butt of ground. His rows were straight, clearly he had a good eye. His cut appeared to be deep, by the rich black of the upturned tilth. True, he had somewhat sprayed soil over the border paths, but he had also ferreted out a twig broom from the shed, and was busy brushing back the spilled earth to where it belonged. He looked up a little defensively at Cadfael, flicking a glance towards the spade he had left lying.

'I've blunted the iron edge against a stone,' he said, and dropped his broom to up-end the spade and run his fingers gingerly along the metal rim that bound the wood. 'I'll hammer it out fine before I leave it. There's a hammer in the shed there, and your water trough has a good wide rim to the stone. Though I was aiming at two rows more before the light goes.'

'Son,' said Cadfael heartily, 'you've already done more than ever I expected of you. As for the spade, that edge has been replaced three times at least since the tool was made, and I know well enough it's due for a fourth sheathing very soon. If you think it will do yet a while, at least to finish this task, then beat if out again by all means, but then put it away, and wash, and come to Vespers.'

Benet looked up from the dented edge, suddenly aware of cautious praise, and broke into the broadest and most unguarded grin Cadfael could ever recall seeing, and the speckled, limpid light blazed up in his trout-stream eyes.

'I'll do, then?' he said, between simple pleasure and subtle impudence, flushed and exhilarated with his own energy; and added with unwary honesty: 'I've hardly had a spade in my hands before.'

'Now that,' said Cadfael, straight faced, and eyeing with interest the form and trim of the hands that jutted a little too far from the outgrown sleeves, 'that I never would have suspected.'

'I've worked mostly with –' Benet began in slight haste.

'. . . with horses. Yes, I know! Well, you match today's effort tomorrow, and tomorrow's the next day, and yes, you'll do.'

Cadfael went to Vespers with his mind's eye full of the jaunty figure of his new labourer, striding away to beat out the dented iron edge of the spade into even sharpness, and his ears were still stretched to catch the whistled tune, certainly not liturgical in character, to which Benet's large young feet in their scuffed shoes and borrowed pattens kept time.

'Father Ailnoth was installed in his cure this morning,' said Cadfael, coming fresh from the induction on the second day. 'You didn't want to attend?'

'I?' Benet straightened up over his spade in ingenuous surprise. 'No, why should I? I've got my work here, he can take care of his without any help from me. I hardly knew the man until we set off to come here. Why, did all go well?'

'Yes – oh, yes, all went well. His sermon was perhaps a little harsh on poor sinners,' said Cadfael, doubtfully pondering. 'No doubt he wanted to begin by showing his zeal at the outset. The rein can always be slackened later, when priest and people come to know each other better, and know where they stand. It's never easy for a younger man and a stranger to follow one old and accustomed. The old shoe comforts, the new pinches. But given time enough, the new comes to be the old, and fits as gently.'

It seemed that Benet had very quickly developed the ability to read between lines where his new master was concerned. He stood gazing earnestly at Cadfael with a slight frown, his curly head on one side, his smooth brown forehead creased in unaccustomed gravity, as if he had been brought up without warning against some unforeseen question, and was suddenly aware that he ought to have been giving thought to it long ago, if he had not been totally preoccupied with some other enterprise of his own.

'Aunt Diota has been with him over three years,' he said consideringly, 'and she's never made any complaint of him, as far as I know. I only rubbed shoulders with him on the way here, and I was thankful to him for bringing me. Not a man a servant like me could be easy with, but I minded my tongue and did what he bade me, and he was fair enough in his dealings with me.' Benet's buoyancy returned like a gust

35

of the western wind, blowing doubts away. 'Ah, here is he as raw in his new work as I am in mine, but he sets out to cudgel his way through, and I have the good sense to worm my way in gently. Let him alone, and he'll get his feet to the ground.'

He was right, of course, a new man comes unmeasured and uneasy into a place not yet mellowed to him, and must be given time to breathe, and listen to the breathing of others. But Cadfael went to his own work with fretting memories of a homily half frenetic dream, half judgement day, eloquently phrased, beginning with the pure air of a scarcely accessible heaven, and ending with the anatomy of a far-too-visual hell.

'. . . that hell which is an island, for ever circled by four seas, the guardian dragons of the condemned. The sea of bitterness, whose every wave burns more white-hot than the mainland fires of hell itself; the sea of rebellion, which at every stroke of swimmer or rower casts the fugitive back into the fire; the sea of despair, in which every barque founders, and every swimmer sinks like a stone. And last, the sea of penitence, composed of all the tears of all the damned, by which alone, for the very few, escape is possible, since a single tear of Our Lord over sinners once fell into the fiery flood, and permeated, cooled and calmed the entire ocean for such as reach the perfection of remorse . . .'

A narrow and terrifying mercy, thought Cadfael, stirring a balsam for the chests of the old, imperfect men in the infirmary, human and fallible like himself, and not long for this world. Hardly mercy at all!

Chapter Three

The first small cloud that showed in the serene sky of the Foregate came when Aelgar, who had always worked the field strips of the priest's glebe, and cared for the parish bull and the parish boar, came with a grievance to Erwald the wheelwright, who was provost of the Foregate, rather in anxiety than in any spirit of rebellion, complaining that his new master had raised doubts about whether his servant was free or villein. For there was one strip in the more distant fields which was in mild dispute at the time of Father Adam's death, and the tenure had not been agreed between priest and man when Adam died. Had he lived there would have been an amicable arrangement, since Adam certainly had no greed in his make-up, and there was a fair claim on Aelgar's part through his mother. But Father Ailnoth, unswervingly exact, had insisted rather that the case should come to court, and further, had said outright that in the King's court Aelgar would have no standing, since he was not free, but villein.

'And everyone knows,' said Aelgar, fretting, 'that I'm a free man and always have been, but he says I have villein kin, for my uncle and my cousin have a yardland in the manor of Worthin, and hold it by customary services, and that's the proof. And true enough, for my father's younger brother, being landless, took the yardland gladly when it fell vacant, and agreed to do service for it, but for all that he was born free, like all my kin. It's not that I grudge him or the church that strip, if it's justly his, but how if he bring case to prove me a villein and no free man?'

'He'll not do that,' said Erwald comfortably, 'for it would never stand if he did. And why should he want to do you wrong? He's a stickler for the letter of the law, you'll find, but nothing more than that. Why, every soul in the parish would testify. I'll tell him so, and he'll hear reason.'

But the tale had gone round before nightfall.

The second small blot in the clear sky was an urchin with a broken head, who admitted, between sniffs and sobs, that he and a few more of his age had been playing a somewhat rumbustious ball game against the wall of the priest's house, a clear, windowless wall well suited for the purpose, and that they had naturally made a certain amount of noise in the process. But so they had many times before, and Father Adam had never done worse than shake a tolerant fist at them, and grin, and finally shoo them away like chickens. This time a tall black figure had surged out of the house crying anathema at them and brandishing a great long staff, and even their startled speed had not been enough to bring them off without damage. Two or three had bad bruises to show for it, and this unfortunate had taken a blow on the head that all but stunned him, and left him with a broken wound that bled alarmingly for a while, as head wounds do.

'I know they can be imps of Satan,' said Erwald to Brother Cadfael, when the child had been soothed and bandaged and lugged away by an indignant mother, 'and many a time I expect you and I have clouted a backside or boxed an ear, but not with a great walking-staff like that one he carries.'

'That could well have been an unlucky stroke that was never meant to land,' said Cadfael. 'But I wouldn't say he'll ever be as easy on the scamps as Father Adam was. They'd best learn to stay out of his way, or mind their manners within reach of him.'

It was soon plain that the boys thought so, too, for there were no more noisy games outside the small house at the end of the alley, and when the tall, black-clad figure was seen stalking down the Foregate, cloak flying like a crow's wings in time to his impetuous stride, the children melted away to safe distances, even when they were about blameless business.

It certainly could not be said that Father Ailnoth neglected his duties. He was meticulous in observing the hours, and let nothing interrupt his saying of the office, he preached somewhat stern sermons, conducted his services reverently, visited the sick, exhorted the backsliding. His comfort to the ailing was austere, even chilling, and his penances heavier than those to which his flock was accustomed, but he did all that his cure required of him. He also took jealous care of all the perquisites of his office, tithe and tilth, to the extent that one of his neighbours in the fields was complaining of having half his headland ploughed up, and Aelgar was protesting that he had been ordered to plough more closely, for the waste of ground was blameworthy.

The few boys who had been learning a smattering of letters from Father Adam, and had continued their lessons under his successor, grew less and less willing to attend, and muttered to their parents that they were beaten now for the least error, let alone a real offence.

'It was a mistake,' said Brother Jerome loftily, 'ever to let them run wild, as Father Adam did. They feel a proper curb now as affliction, instead of fair usage. What says the Rule on this head? That boys or youths who cannot yet understand how great a punishment excommunication is, must be punished for their offences either by fasting, or by sharp stripes, for their own good. The priest does very properly by them.'

'I cannot regard a simple mistake in letters,' retorted Brother Paul, up in arms for lads no older than his own charges, 'as an offence. Offence argues a will to offend, and these children answer as best they know, having no will but to do well.'

'The offence,' said Jerome pompously, 'is in the neglect and inattention which caused them to be imperfect in answering. Those who attend diligently will be able to answer without fault.'

'Not when they are already afraid,' snapped Brother Paul, and fled the argument for fear of his own temper. Jerome had a way of presenting his pious face as a target, and Paul, who like most big, powerful men could be astonishingly gentle and tender with the helpless, like his youngest pupils, was only too well aware of what his fists could do to an opponent of his own size, let alone a puny creature like Jerome.

It was more than a week before the matter came to the notice of Abbot Radulfus, and even then it was a relatively minor complaint that set the affair in motion. For Father Ailnoth had publicly accused Jordan Achard, the Foregate baker, of delivering short-weight loaves, and Jordan, rightly pricked in his professional pride, meant to rebut the charge at all costs.

'And a lucky man he is,' said Erwald the provost heartily, 'that he's charged with the one thing every soul in the Foregate will swear is false, for he gives just measure and always has, if he does nothing else justly in his life. If he'd been charged with fathering one or two of the recent bastards in these parts, he'd have had good cause to sing very low. But he bakes good bread, and never cheats on the weight. And how the priest came by this error is a mystery, but Jordan wants blood for it, and he has a fluent mouth on him that might well speak up usefully for others less bold.'

So it was that the provost of the Foregate, backed by Jordan the baker and one or two more of the notables of the parish, came to ask audience of Abbot Radulfus in chapter on the eighteenth day of December.

'I have asked you here into private with me,' said the abbot, when they had withdrawn at his request into the parlour in his lodging, 'so that the daily duties of the brothers may not be disrupted. For I see that you have much to discuss, and I would like you to speak freely. Now we have time enough. Master Provost, you have my attention. I desire the prosperity and happiness of the Foregate, as you do.'

His very use of the courtesy title, to which Erwald had no official right, was meant as an invitation, and as such accepted.

'Father Abbot,' began Erwald earnestly, 'we are come to you thus because we are not altogether easy at the rule of our new priest. Father Ailnoth has his duties in the church, and performs them faithfully, and there we have no complaint of him. But where he moves among us in the parish we are not happy with his dealings. He has called into question whether Aelgar, who works for him, is villein or free, and has not asked of us, who know very well he is a free man. He has also caused Aelgar to plough up a part of the headland of his neighbour Eadwin, without Eadwin's knowledge or leave. He has accused Master Jordan, here, of giving short weight, while all of us here know that is false. Jordan is known for good bread and good measure.'

'That is truth,' said Jordan emphatically. 'I rent my bakery ovens from the abbey, it is on your land I work, you have known me for years, that I take pride in my bread.'

'You have that right,' agreed Radulfus, 'it is good bread. Go on, Master Provost, there is more to tell.'

'My lord, there is,' said Erwald, very gravely now. 'You may have heard with what strict dealing Father Ailnoth keeps his school. The same severity he uses towards the boys of the parish, wherever he sees them gathered, if they put a foot aside – and you know that the young are liable to folly. He is too free with his blows, he has done violence where it was not called for, not by our measure. The children are afraid of him. That is not good, though not everyone has patience with children. But the women are frightened, too. He preaches such dire things, they are afraid of hell.'

'There is no need to fear,' said the abbot, 'unless by reason of a consciousness of sin. I do not think we have here in the parish such great sinners.'

'No, my lord, but women are tender and easily frightened. They look within for sins they may have committed, unknowing. They are no longer sure what is sin and what is not, so they dare not breathe without wondering if they do wrong. But there is more still.'

'I am listening,' said the abbot.

'My lord, there's a decent poor man of this parish, Centwin, whose wife Elen bore a very weakly child, a boy, four days ago. It was about Sext when the baby was born, and it was so small and feeble, they were sure it must die, and Centwin ran quickly to the priest's house, and begged him to come and baptise the boy before he died, that his soul might be saved. And Father Ailnoth sent out word that he was at his devotions, and could not come until he had completed the office. Centwin begged him, but he would not interrupt his prayers. And when he did go, Father, the baby was dead.'

The small, chill silence seemed to bring down a looming darkness on the panelled room.

'Father, he would not give the child Christian burial, because it was not baptised. He said it could not come within the hallowed ground, though he would say what prayers he could at its burial – which was in a grave outside the pale. The place I can show.'

Abbot Radulfus said with infinite heaviness: 'He was within his rights.'

'His rights! What of the child's rights? It might have been christen soul if he had come when he was called for.'

'He was within his rights,' said Radulfus again, inexorably but with deep detestation. 'The office is sacrosanct.'

'So is the newborn soul,' said Erwald, remorselessly eloquent.

'You say well. And God hears us both. There can and shall be dispensation. If you have more to tell, go on, tell me all.'

'My lord, there was a girl of this parish – Eluned – very beautiful. Not like other girls, wild as a hare. Everyone knew her. God knows she never harmed a soul but herself, the creature! My lord, she could not say no to men. Time and again she went with this one or that, but always she came back, as wild returning as going, in tears, and made her confession, and swore amendment. And meant it! But she never could keep it, a lad would look at her and sigh. . . . Father Adam always took her back, confessed her, gave her penance, and afterwards absolution. He knew she could not

42

help it. And she as kind a creature to man or child or beast as ever breathed – too kind!'

The abbot sat still and silent, foreseeing what was to come.

'Last month she bore a child. When she was delivered and recovered she came, as she always came, mad with shame, to make her confession. He refused her countenance. He told her she had broken every promise of amendment, and so she had, but still . . . He would not give her penance, because he would not take her word, and so he refused her absolution. And when she came humbly to enter the church and hear Mass, he turned her away, and shut the door against her. Publicly and loudly he did it, in front of all.'

There was a long and deep silence before the abbot asked, perforce: 'What became of her?' For clearly she was already in the past, an outcast shade.

'They took her out of the mill-pond, my lord. By good fortune she had drifted down to the brook, and those who drew her out were from the town, and did not know her, so they took her with them back to their own parish, and the priest of Saint Chad's has buried her. It was not clear how she came to drown, it was taken for accident.'

Though of course everyone knew it was none. That was clear in look and voice. Despair is deadly sin. Then what of the record of those who deal out despair?

'Leave all this in my hands,' said Abbot Radulfus. 'I will speak to Father Ailnoth.'

There was no trace of guilt, trepidation or want of assurance in the long, austere, handsome face that confronted Abbot Radulfus across the desk in his parlour, after Mass. The man stood quite erect and still, with hands folded at ease and face invincibly calm.

'Father Abbot, if I may speak freely, the souls of my cure had been long neglected, to their own ruin. The garden is full of weeds, they starve and strangle the good grain. I am pledged to do whatever is needed to bring a clean crop, and so I must and will endeavour. I can do no other. The child spared will be the man spoiled. As for the matter of Eadwin's headland, it has been shown me that I have removed his boundary stone. That was in error, and the error has been made good. I have replaced the stone and drawn my own bounds short of it. I would not possess myself of one hand's breadth of land that belonged to another man.'

And that was surely truth. Not a hand's breadth of land nor a penny in money. Nor let go of one or the other that belonged to him. The bare razor of justice was his measure.

'I am less concerned for a yard of headland,' said the abbot drily, 'than for matters that touch a man's being even more nearly. Your man Aelgar was born free, is free man now, and so are his uncle and cousin, and if they take steps to assert it there will be no man query it hereafter. They assumed such customary duties as they do by way of payment for a piece of land, there is no disfranchisement, no more than when a man pays in money.'

'So I have found by enquiry,' said Ailnoth imperturbably, 'and have said as much to him.'

'Then that was properly done. But it would have been better to enquire first and accuse afterwards.'

'My lord, no just man should resent the appeal to justice. I am new among these people, I heard of the kinsmen's land, that it was held by villein service. It was my duty to find out the truth, and it was honest to speak first to the man himself.'

Which was true enough, if not kindly, and it seemed he had acknowledged the truth against himself, once established, with the same steely integrity. But what is to be done with such a man, among the common, fallible run of humanity? Radulfus went on to graver matters.

'The child that was born to the man Centwin and his wife, and lived barely an hour. . . . The man came to you, urging haste, since the baby was very feeble and likely to die. You did not go with him to give it Christian baptism, and since your ministration came too late, as I hear, you denied the infant burial in consecrated ground. Why did you not go at once when you were called, and with all haste?'

'Because I had but just begun the office. My lord, I never have broken off my devotions according to my vows, and never will, for any cause, though it were my own death. Until I had completed the act of worship I could not go. As soon as it was ended, I did go. I could not know the child would die so soon. But if I had known, still I could not have cut short the worship I owe.'

'There are other obligations you owe no less,' said Radulfus with some asperity. 'There are times when it is needful to make a choice between duties, and yours, I think, is first to the souls of those within your care. You chose rather the perfection of your own personal worship, and consigned the child to a grave outside the pale: Was that well done?'

'My lord,' said Ailnoth, unflinching, and with the high and smouldering gleam of self-justification in his black eyes, 'as I hold, it was. I will not go aside from the least iota of my service where the sacred office is concerned. My own soul and all others must bow to that.'

'Even the soul of the most innocent, new come into the world, the most defenceless of God's creatures?'

'My lord, you know well that the letter of divine law does not permit the burial of unchristened creatures within the pale. I keep the rules by which I am bound. I can do no other. God will know where to find Centwin's babe, if his mercy extends to him, in holy ground or base.'

After its merciless fashion it was a good answer. The abbot pondered, eyeing the stony, assured face.

'The letter of the rule is much, I grant you, but the spirit is more. And you might well have jeopardised your own soul to ensure that of a newborn child. An office interrupted can be completed without sin, if the cause be urgent enough. And there is also the matter of the girl Eluned, who went to her death after – I say after, mark, I do not say because! – you turned her away from the church. It is a grave thing to refuse confession and penance even to the greatest sinner.'

'Father Abbot,' said Ailnoth, with the first hot spurt of

passion, immovable in righteousness, 'where there is no penitence there can be neither penance nor absolution. The woman had pleaded penitence and vowed amendment time after time, and never kept her word. I have heard from others all her reputation, and it is past amendment. I could not in conscience confess her, for I could not take her word. If there is no truth in the act of contrition, there is no merit in confession, and to absolve her would have been deadly sin. A whore past recovery! I do not repent me, whether she died or no. I would do again what I did. There is no compromise with the pledges by which I am bound.'

'There will be no compromise with the answer you must make for two deaths,' said Radulfus solemnly, 'if God should take a view different from yours. I bid you recall, Father Ailnoth, that you are summoned to call not the righteous, but sinners to repentance, the weak, the fallible, those who go in fear and ignorance, and have not your pure advantage. Temper your demands to their abilities, and be less severe on those who cannot match your perfection.' He paused there, for it was meant as irony, to bite, but the proud, impervious face never winced, accepting the accolade. 'And be slow to lay your hand upon the children,' he said, 'unless they offend of malicious intent. To error we are all liable, even you.'

'I study to do right,' said Ailnoth, 'as I have always, and always shall.' And he went away with the same confident step, vehement and firm, the skirts of his gown billowing like wings in the wind of his going.

'A man abstemious, rigidly upright, inflexibly honest, ferociously chaste,' said Radulfus in private to Prior Robert. 'A man with every virtue, except humility and human kindess. That is what I have brought upon the Foregate, Robert. And now what are we to do about him?'

Dame Diota Hammet came on the twenty-second day of December to the gatehouse of the abbey with a covered basket, and asked meekly for her nephew Benet, for whom she had brought a cake for his Christmas, and a few honey buns from her festival baking. The porter, knowing her for the parish priest's housekeeper, directed her through to the garden, where Benet was busy clipping the last straggly growth from the box hedges.

Hearing their voices, Cadfael looked out from his workshop, and divining who this matronly woman must be, was about to return to his mortar when he was caught by some delicate shade in their greeting. A matter-of-fact affection, easy-going and undemonstrative, was natural between aunt and nephew, and what he beheld here hardly went beyond that, but for all that there was a gloss of tenderness and almost deference in the woman's bearing towards her young kinsman, and an unexpected, childish grace in the warmth with which he embraced her. True, he was already known for a young man who did nothing by halves, but here were certainly aunt and nephew who did not take each other for granted.

Cadfael withdrew to his work again and left them their privacy. A comely, well-kept woman was Mistress Hammet, with decent black clothing befitting a priest's housekeeper, and a dark shawl over her neat, greying hair. Her oval face, mildly sad in repose, brightened vividly in greeting the boy, and then she looked no more than forty years old, and perhaps, indeed, she was no more. Benet's mother's sister, wondered Cadfael? If so, he took after his father, for there was very little resemblance here. Well, it was none of his business!

Benet came bounding into the workshop to empty the basket of its good things, spreading them out on the wooden bench. 'We're in luck, Brother Cadfael, for she's as good a cook as you'd find in the King's own kitchen. You and I can eat like princes.'

And he was off again as blithely to restore the empty basket. Cadfael looked out after him through the open door, and saw him hand over, besides the basket, some small thing he drew from the breast of his cotte. She took it, nodding earnestly, unsmiling, and the boy stooped and kissed her cheek. She smiled then. He had a way with him, no question. She turned and went away, and left him looking after her for a long moment, before he also turned, and came back to the workshop. The engaging grin came back readily to his face.

'"On no account,"' quoted Cadfael, straight-faced, '"may a monk accept small presents of any kind, from his parents or anyone else, without the abbot's permission." That, sweet son, is in the Rule.'

'Lucky you, then, and lucky I,' said the boy gaily, 'that I've taken no vows. She makes the best honey cakes ever I tasted.' And he sank even white teeth into one of them, and reached to offer another to Cadfael.

'". . . nor may the brethren exchange them, one with another,"' said Cadfael, and accepted the offering. 'Lucky, indeed! Though I transgress in accepting, you go sinless in offering. Have you quite abandoned your inclination to the cloistered life, then?'

'Me?' said the youth, startled out of his busy munching, and open-mouthed. 'When did I ever profess any?'

'Not you, lad, but your sponsor on your account, when he asked work for you here.'

'Did he say that of me?'

'He did. Not positively promising it, mark you, but holding out the hope that you might settle to it one day. I grant you I've never seen much sign of it.'

Benet thought that over for a moment, while he finished his cake and licked the sticky crumbs from his fingers. 'No doubt he was anxious to get rid of me, and thought it might make me more welcome here. My face was never in any great favour with him – too much given to smiling, maybe. No, not even you will pen me in here for very long, Cadfael. When the time comes I'll be on my way. But while I'm here,' he said, breaking into the bountiful smile that might well strike an ascetic as far too frivolous, 'I'll do my fair share of the work.'

And he was off back to his box hedge, swinging the shears in one large, easy hand, and leaving Cadfael gazing after him with a very thoughtful face.

Chapter Four

Dame Diota Hammet presented herself later that afternoon at a house near Saint Chad's church, and asked timidly for the lord Ralph Giffard. The servant who opened the door to her looked her up and down and hesitated, never having seen her before.

'What's your business with him, mistress? Who sends you?'

'I'm to bring him this letter,' said Diota submissively, and held out a small rolled leaf fastened with a seal. 'And to wait for an answer, if my lord will be so good.'

He was in two minds about taking it from her hand. It was a small and irregularly shaped slip of parchment, with good reason, since it was one of the discarded edges from a leaf Brother Anselm had trimmed to shape and size for a piece of music, two days since. But the seal argued matter of possible importance, even on so insignificant a missive. The servant was still hesitating when a girl came out into the porch at his back, and seeing a woman unknown but clearly respectable, stayed to enquire curiously what was to do. She accepted the scroll readily enough, and knew the seal. She looked up with startled, intent blue eyes into Diota's face, and abruptly handed the scroll back to her.

'Come in, and deliver this yourself. I'll bring you to my step-father.'

The master of the house was sitting by a comfortable fire in a small solar, with wine at his elbow and a deerhound coiled about his feet. A big, ruddy, sinewy man of fifty, balding and bearded, very spruce in his dress and only just beginning to put on a little extra flesh after an active life, he looked what he was, the lord of two or three country manors and this town house, where he preferred to spend his Christmas in comfort. He looked up at Diota, when the girl presented her, with complete incomprehension, but he comprehended all too well when he looked at the seal that fastened the parchment. He asked no questions, but sent the girl for his clerk, and listened intently as the content was read to him, in so low a voice that it was plain the clerk understood how dangerous its import could be. He was a small, withered man, grown old in Giffard's service, and utterly trustworthy. He made an end, and watched his master's face anxiously.

'My lord, send nothing in writing! Word of mouth is safer, if you want to reply. Words said can be denied, to write them would be folly.'

Ralph sat pondering for a while in silence, and eyeing the unlikely messenger, who stood patiently and uneasily waiting.

'Tell him,' he said at last, 'that I have received and understood his message.'

She hesitated, and ventured at last to ask: 'Is that all, my lord?'

'It's enough! The less said the better, for him and for me.'

The girl, who had remained unobtrusive but attentive in a corner of the room, followed Diota out to the shadow of the porch, with doors closed behind them.

'Mistress,' she said softly in Diota's ear, 'where is he to be found – this man who sent you?'

By the brief, blank silence and the doubtful face of the older woman she understood her fears, and made impatient haste to allay them, her voice low and vehement. 'I mean him no harm, God knows! My father was of the same party – did you not see how well I knew the seal? You can trust me, I won't say word to any, nor to him, either, but I want to know how I may know him, where I may find him, in case of need.'

'At the abbey,' said Diota as softly and hurriedly, making up her mind. 'He's working in the garden, by the name of Benet, under the herbalist brother.'

'Oh, Brother Cadfael – I know him!' said the girl, breathing satisfaction. 'He treated me once for a bad fever, when I was ten years old, and he came to help my mother, three Christmases ago, when she fell into her last illness. Good, I know where his herbarium is. Go now, quickly!'

She watched Diota scurry hastily out of the small courtyard, and then closed the door and went back to the solar, where Giffard was sitting sunk in anxious consideration, heavy-browed and sombre.

'Shall you go to this meeting?'

He had the letter still in his hand. Once already he had made an impulsive motion towards the fire, to thrust the parchment into it and be rid of it, but then had drawn back again, rolled it carefully and hid it in the breast of his cotte. She took that for a sign favourable to the sender, and was pleased. It was no surprise that he did not give her a direct answer. This was a serious business and needed thought, and in any case he never paid any great heed to his step-daughter, either to confide in her or to regulate her actions. He was indulgent rather out of tolerant indifference than out of affection.

'Say no word of this to anyone,' he said. 'What have I to gain by keeping such an appointment? And everything to lose! Have not your family and mine lost enough already by loyalty to that cause? How if he should be followed to the mill?'

'Why should he be? No one has any suspicion of him. He's accepted at the abbey as a labourer in the gardens, calling himself Benet. He's vouched for. Christmas Eve, and by night, there'll be no one abroad but those already in the church. Where's the risk? It was a good time to choose. And he needs help.'

'Well. . . .' said Ralph, and drummed his fingers irreso-lutely on the small cylinder in the breast of his cotte. 'We have two days yet, we'll watch and wait until the time comes.'

Benet was sweeping up the brushings from the hedge, and whistling merrily over the work, when he heard brisk, light steps stirring the moist gravel on the path behind him, and turned to behold a young woman in a dark cloak and hood advancing upon him from the great court. A small, slender girl of erect and confident bearing, the outline of her swathed form softened and blurred by the faint mist of a still day, and the hovering approach of dusk. Not until she was quite near to him and he had stepped deferentially aside to give her passage could he see clearly the rosy, youthful face within the shadow of the hood, a rounded face with apple-blossom skin, a resolute chin, and a mouth full and firm in its generosity of line, and coloured like half-open roses. Then what light remained gathered into the harebell blue of her wide-set eyes, at once soft and brilliant, and he lost sight of everything else. And though he had made way for her to pass him by, and ducked his head to her in a properly servantlike reverence, she did not pass by, but lingered, studying him closely and candidly, with the fearless, innocent stare of a cat. Indeed there was something of the kitten about the whole face, wider at the brow and eyes than its length from brow to chin, tapered and tilted imperiously, as a kitten confronts the world, never having experienced fear. She looked him up and down gravely, and took her time about it, in a solemn inspection that might have been insolent if it had not implied a very serious purpose. Though what interest some noble young woman of the county or well-to-do merchant daughter of the town could have in him was more than Benet could imagine.

Only when she was satisfied of whatever had been in question in her mind did she ask, in a clear, firm voice: 'Are you Brother Cadfael's new helper here?'

'Yes, my lady,' said the dutiful labourer bashfully, shuffling his feet and somehow even contriving a blush that sat rather oddly on so positive and cheerful a countenance.

She looked at the trimmed hedge and the newly weeded and manured flower beds, and again at him, and for a dazzling instant he thought she smiled, but in the flicker of an eyelash she was solemn again.

'I came to ask Brother Cadfael for some herbs for my kitchen forcemeats. Do you know were I shall find him?'

'He's in his workshop within,' said Benet. 'Please to walk through into the walled garden there.'

'I remember the way,' she said, and inclined her head to him graciously, as noble to simple, and swept away from him through the open gate into the walled enclosure of the herbarium.

It was almost time for Vespers, and Benet could well have quit his labours and gone to make himself ready, but he prolonged his sweeping quite unnecessarily, gathering the brushings into a pile of supererogatory neatness, scattering them a little and massing them again, in order to get another close glimpse of her when she came blithely back with a bunch of dried herbs loosely wrapped in a cloth and carried carefully in her hands. She passed him this time without a glance, or seemed to do so, but still he had the feeling that those wide and wide-set eyes with their startling blueness took him in methodically in passing. The hood had slipped back a little from her head, and showed him a coiled braid of hair of an indefinable spring colour, like the young fronds of bracken when they are just unfolding, a soft light brown with tones of green in the shadows. Or hazel withies, perhaps! Hazel eyes are no great rarity, but how many women can boast of hazel hair?

She was gone, the hem of her cloak whisking round the box hedge and out of his sight. Benet forsook his broom in haste, left his pile of brushings lying, and went to pick Brother Cadfael's brains.

'Who was that lady?' he asked, point-blank.

'Is that a proper question for a postulant like you to be asking?' said Cadfael placidly, and went on cleaning and putting away his pestle and mortar.

Benet made a derisive noise, and interposed his sturdy person to confront Cadfael eye to eye, with no pretence whatsoever to notions of celibacy. 'Come, you know her, or at least she knows you. Who is she?'

'She spoke to you?' Cadfael wondered, interested.

'Only to ask me where she would find you. Yes, she spoke to me!' he said, elated. 'Yes, she stopped and looked me up and down, the creature, as though she found herself in need of a page, and thought I might do, given a little polishing. Would I do for a lady's page, Cadfael?'

'What's certain,' said Cadfael tolerantly, 'is that you'll never do for a monk. But no, I wouldn't say a lady's service is your right place, either.' He did not add: 'Unless on level terms!' but that was what was in his mind. At this moment the boy had shed all pretence of being a poor widow's penniless kinsman, untutored and awkward. That was no great surprise. There had been little effort spent on the imposture here in the garden for a week past, though the boy could reassume it at a moment's notice with others, and was still the rustic simpleton in Prior Robert's patronising presence.

'Cadfael . . .' Benet took him cajolingly by the shoulders and held him, tilting his curly head coaxingly, with a wilfully engaging intimacy. Given the occasion, he was well aware he could charm the birds from the trees. Nor did he have any difficulty in weighing up elder sympathisers who must once have shared much the same propensities. 'Cadfael, I may never speak to her again, I may never see her again – but I can *try*! Who is she?'

'Her name,' said Cadfael, capitulating rather from policy than from compulsion, 'is Sanan Bernières. Her father held a manor in the north-east of the shire, which was confiscated when he fought for his overlord FitzAlan and the Empress at the siege here, and died for it. Her mother married another vassal of FitzAlan, who had suffered his losses, too – the faction holds together, though they're all singing very small and lying very low here now. Giffard spends his winters mainly in his house in Shrewsbury, and since her mother died he brings his step-daughter to preside at his table-head. That's the lady you've seen pass by.'

'And had better let pass by?' said Benet, ruefully smiling in acknowledgement of a plain warning. 'Not for me?' He burst into the glowing grin to which Cadfael was becoming accustomed, and which sometimes gave him such qualms on behalf of his protégé, who was far too rash in the indulgence of his flashing moods. Benet laughed, and flung his arms about his mentor in a bear's hug. 'What will you wager?'

Cadfael freed an arm, without much ado, and held off his boisterous aggressor by a fistful of his thick curls.

'Where you're concerned, you madcap, I would not risk a hair that's left me. But watch your gait, you move out of your part. There are others here have keen eyes.'

'I do know,' said Benet, brought up short and sharp, his smile sobered into gravity. 'I do take care.'

How had they come by this secret and barely expressed understanding? Cadfael wondered as he went to Vespers. A kind of tacit agreement had been achieved, with never a word said of doubt, suspicion or plain, reckless trust. But the changed relationship existed, and was a factor to be reckoned with.

Hugh was gone, riding south for Canterbury in uncustomary state, well escorted and in his finery. He laughed at himself, but would not abate one degree of the dignity that was his due. 'If I come back deposed,' he said, 'at least I'll make a grand departure, and if I come back sheriff still, I'll do honour to the office.'

After his going Christmas seemed already on the doorstep, and there were great preparations to be made for the long night vigil and the proper celebration of the Nativity, and it was past Vespers on Christmas Eve before Cadfael had time to make a brief visit to the town, to spend at least an hour with Aline, and take a gift to his two-year-old godson, a little wooden horse that Martin Bellecote the master-carpenter had made for him, with gaily coloured harness and trappings fit for a knight, made out of scraps of felt and cloth and leather by Cadfael himself.

A soft, sleety rain had fallen earlier, but by that hour in the evening it was growing very cold, and there was frost in the air. The low, moist sky had cleared and grown infinitely tall, there were stars snapping out in it almost audibly, tiny but brilliant. By the morning the roads would be treacherous, and the frozen ruts a peril to wrenched ankles and unwary steps. There were still people abroad in the Foregate, most of them hurrying home by now, either to stoke up the fire and toast their feet, or to make ready for the long night in church. And as Cadfael crossed the bridge towards the town gate, the river in full, silent dark motion below, there was just enough light left to put names to those he met, coming from their shopping laden and in haste to get their purchases home. They exchanged greetings with him as they passed, for he was well known by his shape and his rolling gait even in so dim a light. The voices had the ring of frost about them, echoing like the chime of glass.

And here, striding across the bridge towards the Foregate, just within the compass of the torches burning under the town gate, came Ralph Giffard, on foot. Without the sidelong fall of the torchlight he would not have been recognised, but thus illuminated he was unmistakable. And where could Giffard be going at this time of the evening, and out of the town? Unless he meant to celebrate Christmas at the church of Holy Cross instead of in his own parish of Saint Chad. That was possible, though if so he was over-early. A good number of the wealthier townsfolk would also be making for the abbey this night.

Cadfael went on up the long curve of the Wyle, between the sparkling celestial darkness and the red, warm, earthy torchlight, to Hugh's house close by Saint Mary's church, and in through the courtyard to the hall door. No sooner had he set foot within than the excited imp Giles bore down upon him, yelling, and embraced him cripplingly round the thighs, which was as high as he could reach. To detach him was easy enough. As soon as the small, cloth-wrapped parcel was lowered into his sight he held up his arms for it gleefully, and plumped down in the rushes of the hall floor to unwrap it with cries of delight. But he did not forget, once the first transports were over, to make a rush for his godfather again, and clamber into his lap by the fireside to present him with a moist but fervent kiss in thanks. He had Hugh's self-reliant nature, but something also of his mother's instinctive sweetness.

'I can stay no more than an hour,' said Cadfael, as the boy scrambled down again to play with his new toy. 'I must be back for Compline, and very soon after that begins Matins, and we shall be up all the night until Prime and the dawn Mass.'

'Then at least rest an hour, and take food with me, and stay until Constance fetches my demon there away to his bed. Will you believe,' said Aline, smiling indulgently upon her offspring, 'what he says of this house without Hugh? Though it was Hugh told him what to say. He says he is the man of the house now, and asks how long his father will be away. He's too proud of himself to miss Hugh. It pleases his lordship to be taking his father's place.'

'You'd find his face fall if you told him longer than three or four days,' said Cadfael shrewdly. 'Tell him he's gone for a week, and there'll be tears. But three days? I daresay his pride will last out that long.'

At that moment the boy had no attention to spare for his dignity as lord of the household or his responsibilities as its protector in his father's absence, he was wholly taken up with galloping his new steed through the open plain of rushes, on some heroic adventure with an imaginary rider. Cadfael was left at liberty to sit with Aline, take meat and wine with her, and think and talk about Hugh, his possible reception at Canterbury, and his future, now hanging in the balance.

'He has deserved well of Stephen,' said Cadfael firmly, 'and Stephen is not quite a fool, he's seen too many change their coats, and change them back again when the wind turned. He'll know how to value one who never changed.'

When he noted the sand in the glass and rose to take his leave, he went out from the hall into the bright glitter of frost, and a vault of stars now three times larger than when first they appeared, and crackling with brilliance. The first real frost of the winter. As he made his way cautiously down the Wyle and out at the town gate he was thinking of the hard winter two years earlier, when the boy had been born, and hoping that this winter there would be no such mountainous snows and ferocious winds to drive it.* This night, the eve of the Nativity, hung about the town utterly still and silent, not a breath to temper the bite of the frost. Even the movements of such men as were abroad seemed hushed and almost stealthy, afraid to shake the wonder.

The bridge had a sheen of silver upon it after the earlier fine rain. The river ran dark and still, with too strong a flow for frost to have any hold. A few voices gave him good night as he passed. In the rutted road of the Foregate he began to hurry, fearing he had lingered a little too long. The trees that sheltered the long riverside level of the Gaye loomed like the dark fur of the earth's winter pelt on his left hand, the flat, pale sheen of the mill-pond opened out on his right, beyond the six little abbey houses of grace, three on either side the near end of the water, a narrow path slipping away from the road to serve each modest row. Silver and dark fell behind, he saw the torchlight glow from the gatehouse golden before him.

Still some twenty paces short of the gate he glimpsed a tall black figure sweeping towards him with long, rapid, fierce strides. The sidelong torchlight snatched it into momentary brightness as it strode past, the darkness took it again as it swept by Cadfael without pause or glance, long staff ringing

The Virgin in the Ice.

against the frosty ruts, wide black garments flying, head and shoulders thrusting forward hungrily, long pale oval of face fixed and grim, and for one instant a vagrant light from the opened door of the nearest house by the pool plucked two crimson sparks of fire from the dark pits of the eyes.

Cadfael called a greeting that was neither heeded nor heard. Father Ailnoth swept by, engendering round him the only turbulence in the night's stillness, and was lost in the dark. Like an avenging fury, Cadfael thought later, like a scavenging raven swooping through the Foregate to hunt out little venial sins, and consign the sinners to damnation.

In the church of Saint Chad, Ralph Giffard bent the knee with a satisfactory feeling of a duty done and fences securely mended. He had lost one manor through loyalty to the cause of his overlord FitzAlan and his sovereign, the Empress Maud, and it had taken him a good deal of cautious treading and quiet submission to achieve the successful retention of what remained. He had but one cause that mattered to him now, and that was to preserve his own situation and leave his remaining estate intact to his son. His life had never been threatened, he had not been so deeply involved as to invite death. But possessions are possessions, and he was an ageing man, by no means minded to abandon his lands and flee either abroad, to Normandy or Anjou, where he had no status, or to Gloucester, to take up arms for the liege lady who had already cost him dear. No, better far to sit still, shun every tempter, and forget old allegiance. Only so could he ensure that young Ralph, busy this Christmas happily playing lord of the manor at home, should survive this long conflict for the crown without loss, no matter which of the two claimants finally triumphed.

Ralph welcomed midnight with deep and genuine gratitude for the mercies shown forth upon men, and not least upon Ralph Giffard.

Benet slipped into the abbey church by the parish door, and made his way softly forward towards a spot where he could look through into the choir, and see the monks in their stalls, faintly lit by the yellow sheen of candles and the red glow of the altar lamps. The chanting of psalms came out into the nave muted and mild. Here the lighting was dim, and the cloaked assembly of the Foregate laity shifted and stirred, kneeled and rose again, every man nameless. There was a little while yet to wait before Matins began at the midnight hour, the celebration of God made flesh, virgin-born and wonderful. Why should not the Holy Spirit engender, as fire kindles fire and light light, the necessary instrument of flesh no more than the fuel that renders its substance to provide warmth and enlightenment? He who questions has already denied himself any answer. Benet did not question. He was breathing hard with haste and excitement, and even elation, for risk was meat to him. But once within here, in the obscurity that was at once peopled and isolated, he lost himself in awe, like the child he would never quite outgrow. He found himself a pillar, rather to brace himself by than to hide behind, and laid a hand to the cold stone, and waited, listening. The matched voices, soft as they were, expanded to fill the vault. The stone above, warmed by the music, reflected its arching radiance to the stone below.

He could see Brother Cadfael in his stall, and moved a little to have him more clearly in view. Perhaps he had chosen this spot purely to have in his sights the person most near to him in this place, a man already compromised, already tolerant, and all without any intent, on either part, to invade another's peace of mind. Only a little while, thought Benet, and you shall be free of me. Will you regret it, now and then, if you never again hear of me? And he wondered if he ought to say something clearly, something to be remembered, while there was still time.

A soft voice, just avoiding the sibilance of a whisper, breathed in his ear: 'He did not come?'

Benet turned his head very slowly, entranced and afraid, for surely it could not be the same voice, heard only once before, and briefly, but still causing the strings of his being to vibrate. And she was there, close at his right shoulder, the veritable, the unforgettable she. A dim, reflected light conjured her features out of the dark hood, broad brow, wide-set eyes, deeply blue. 'No,' she said. 'He didn't come!' And having answered herself, she heaved a great sigh. 'I never thought he would. Don't move – don't look round at me.'

He turned his face obediently towards the parish altar again. The soft breath fanned his cheek as she leaned close. 'You don't know who I am, but I know you.'

'I do know you,' said Benet as softly. Nothing more, and even that was uttered like a man in a dream.

Silence for a moment; then she said: 'Brother Cadfael told you?'

'I asked. . . .'

Silence again, with some soft implication of a smile in it, as though he had said something to please her, even distract her for a moment from whatever purpose had brought her here to his side.

'I know you, too. If Giffard is afraid, I am not. If he won't help you, I will. When can we two talk?'

'Now!' he said, suddenly wide awake and grasping with both hands at an opportunity for which he had never dared to hope. 'After Matins some people will be leaving, so may we. All the brothers will be here until dawn. As good a time as any!'

He felt her warm at his back, and knew when she shook softly with silent, excited laughter. 'Where?'

'Brother Cadfael's workshop.' It was the place he knew best as a possible solitude, while its proprietor kept the Christmas vigil here in the church. The brazier in the hut was turfed down to burn slowly through the night, he could easily blow it into life again to keep her warm. Clearly he could not take advantage of this delicate young being's partisan loyalty so far as to put her in peril, but at least this once he could speak with her alone, feast his eyes on her grave, ardent face, share with her the confidences of allies. Something to remember lifelong, if he never saw her again.

'By the south door, through the cloisters,' he said. 'No one will be there to see us tonight.'

The soft, warm breath in his ear said: 'Need we wait? I could slip into the porch now. Matins will be so long tonight. Will you follow?'

And she was away, not waiting for an answer, stealing silently and reverently across the tiles of the nave, and taking station for a few moments where she could be seen to be gazing devoutly in towards the high altar, beyond the chanting in the choir, in case anyone should be taking note of her movements. By that time he would have followed her wherever she chose to lead him. It hurt even to wait patiently the many minutes she delayed, before she chose her moment to withdraw into the darkness of the south porch. When he followed her, by cautious stages, reaching the darkness of the closed doorway with a great heaved breath of relief, he found her waiting with the heavy latch in her hand, motionless against the door. There they waited, close and quivering, for the first jubilant antiphon of Matins, and the triumphant answering cry:

'Christ is born unto us!'

'Oh, come, let us worship!'

Benet set his hand over hers on the massive latch, and lifted it softly as the hymn began. Outside, the night's darkness matched the darkness within. Who was to pay any attention now to two young creatures slipping through the chink of the door into the cold of the night, and cautiously letting the latch slide back into place? There was no one in the cloister, no one in the great court as they crossed it. Whether it was Benet who reached for her hand, or she for his, they rounded the corner of the thick box hedge in the garden hand in hand, and slowed to a walk there, panting and smiling, palms tightly clasped together, their breath a faint silver mist. The vast inverted bowl of sky, dark blue almost to blackness but polished bright and scintillating with stars, poured down upon them a still coldness they did not feel.

Brother Cadfael's timbered hut, solid and squat in the

sheltered enclosure, never quite lost its warmth. Benet closed the door gently behind them, and groped along the little shelf he knew now almost as well as did Cadfael himself, where the tinder box and lamp lay ready to hand. It took him two or three attempts before the charred linen caught at the spark, and let him blow it carefully into a glow. The wick of the lamp put up a tiny, wavering flame that grew into a steady flare, and stood up tall and erect. The leather bellows lay by the brazier, he had only to shift a turf or two and spend a minute industriously pumping, and the charcoal glowed brightly, and accepted a feeding of split wood to burn into a warm hearth.

'He'll know someone has been here,' said the girl, but very tranquilly.

'He'll know I was here,' said Benet, getting up lithely from his knees, his bold, boy's face conjured into summer bronze by the glow from the brazier. 'I doubt if he'll say so. But he may wonder why. And with whom!'

'You've brought other women here?' She tilted her head at him in challenge, abruptly displeased.

'Never any, till now. Never any, hereafter. Unless you so pleasure me a second time,' he said, and stared her down with fiery solemnity.

Some resinous knot in the new wood caught and hissed, sending up a clear, white flame for a moment between them. Across its pale, pure gold the two young faces sprang into mysterious brightness, lit from below, lips parted, eyes rounded in astonished gravity. Each of them stared into a mirror, matched and mated, and could not look away from the unexpected image of love.

Chapter Five

Prime was said at an early hour, after a very short interlude for sleep, and the dawn Mass followed with first light. Almost all the people of the Foregate had long since gone home, and the brothers, dazed with long standing and strung taut with the tensions of music and wonder, filed a little unsteadily up the night stairs to rest briefly before preparing for the day.

Brother Cadfael, stiff with being still for so long a time, felt himself in need rather of movement than of rest. Solitary in the lavatorium, he made unusually leisurely ablutions, shaved with care, and went out into the great court, just in time to see Dame Diota Hammet come hurrying in through the wicket in the gate, stumbling and slipping on the glazed cobbles, clutching her dark cloak about her, and gazing round in evident agitation. A furry fringe of hoar frost had formed on the collar of her cloak from her breath. Every outline of wall or bush or branch was silvered with the same glittering whiteness.

The porter had come out to greet her and ask her business, but she had observed Prior Robert emerging from the cloisters, and made for him like a homing bird, making him so low and unwary a reverence that she almost fell on her knees.

'Father Prior, my master – Father Ailnoth – has he been all night in the church with you?'

'I have not seen him,' said Robert, startled, and put out a hand in haste to help her keep her feet, for the rounded stones were wickedly treacherous. He held on to the arm he had grasped, and peered concernedly into her face. 'What is amiss? Surely he has his own Mass to take care of soon. By this time he should be robing. I should not interrupt him now, unless for some very grave reason. What is your need?'

'He is not there,' she said abruptly. 'I have been up to see. Cynric is there waiting, ready, but my master has not come.'

Prior Robert had begun to frown, certain that this silly woman was troubling him for no good reason, and yet made uneasy by her agitation. 'When did you see him last? You must know when he left his house.'

'Last evening, before Compline,' she said bleakly.

'What? And has not been back since then?'

'No, Father. He never came home all night. I thought he might have come to take part in your night offices, but no one has seen him even here. And as you say, by now he should be robing for his own Mass. But he is not there!'

Halted at the foot of the day stairs, Cadfael could not choose but overhear, and having overheard, inevitably recalled the ominous black-winged bird swooping along the Foregate towards the bridge at very much the same hour, according to Diota, when Ailnoth had left his own house. On what punitive errand, Cadfael wondered? And where could those raven wings have carried him, to cause him to fail of his duty on such a festal day?

'Father,' he said, coming forward with unwary haste, slithering on the frosty cobbles, 'I met the priest last night as I was coming back from the town to be in time for Compline. Not fifty paces from the gatehouse here, going towards the bridge, and in a hurry.'

Prior Robert looked round, frowning, at this unsolicited witness, and gnawed a lip in doubt how to proceed. 'He did not speak to you? You don't know where he was bound in such haste?'

'No. I spoke to him,' said Cadfael drily, 'but he was too intent to mark me. No, I have no notion where he was bound. But it was he. I saw him pass the light of the torches under the gate. No mistaking him.'

The woman was staring at him now with bruised, hollow eyes and still face, and the hood had slipped back from her forehead unnoticed, and showed a great leaden bruise on her left temple, broken at the centre by a wavering line of dried blood.

'You're hurt!' said Cadfael, asking no leave, and put back the folds of cloth from her head and turned her face to the dawning light. 'This is a bad blow you've suffered, it needs tending. How did you come by it?'

She shrank a little from his touch, and then submitted with a resigned sigh. 'I came out in the night, anxious about him, to see if there was anyone stirring, or any sign of him. The doorstone was frozen, I fell and struck my head. I've washed it well, it's nothing.'

Cadfael took her hand and turned up to view a palm rasped raw in three or four grazes, took up its fellow and found it marked almost as brutally. 'Well, perhaps you saved yourself worse by putting out these hands. But you must let me dress them for you, and your brow, too.'

Prior Robert stood gazing beyond them, pondering what it was best to do. 'Truly I wonder . . . If Father Ailnoth went out at that hour, and in such haste, may not he also have fallen, somewhere, and so injured himself that he's lying helpless? The frost was already setting in. . . .'

'It was,' said Cadfael, remembering the glassy sheen on the steep slope of the Wyle, and the icy ring of his own steps on the bridge. 'And sharply! And I would not say he was minding his steps when I saw him.'

'Some charitable errand. . .' murmured Robert anxiously. 'He would not spare himself. . . .'

No, neither himself nor any other soul! But true enough, those hasty steps might well have lunged into slippery places.

'If he has lain all night helpless in the cold,' said Robert, 'he may have caught his death. Brother Cadfael, do you tend to this lady, do whatever is needful, and I will go and speak to

Father Abbot. For I think we had best call all the brothers and lay brothers together, and set in hand a hunt for Father Ailnoth, wherever he may be.'

In the dim, quiet shelter of the workshop in the garden Cadfael sat his charge down on the bench against the wall, and turned to his brazier, to uncover it for the day. All the winter he kept it thus turfed overnight, to be ready at short notice if needed, the rest of the year he let it out, since it could easily be rekindled. None of his brews within here required positive warmth, but there were many among them that would not take kindly to frost.

The thick turves now damping it down were almost fresh, though neatly placed, and the fire beneath them live and comforting. Someone had been here during the night, and someone who knew how to lay his hand on the lamp and the tinder without disturbing anything else, and how to tend the fire to leave it much as he had found it. Young Benet had left few traces, but enough to set his signature to the nocturnal invasion. Even by night, it seemed, he practised very little dissembling where Cadfael was concerned, he was intent rather on leaving everything in order than on concealing his intrusion.

Cadfael warmed water in a pan, and diluted a lotion of betony, comfrey and daisy to cleanse the broken bruise on her forehead and the scored grazes in both palms, scratches that ran obliquely from the wrist to the root of the forefinger and thumb, torn by the frozen and rutted ground. She submitted to his ministrations with resigned dignity, her eyes veiled.

'That's a heavy fall you had,' said Cadfael, wiping away the dried line of blood from her temple.

'I was not minding myself,' she said, so simply that he knew it for plain truth. 'I am not of any importance.'

Her face, seen thus below him as he fingered her forehead, was a long oval, with fine, elongated features. Large, arched eyelids hid her eyes, her mouth was well shaped and generous but drooping with weariness. She braided her greying hair severely and coiled it behind her head. Now that she had told what she had come to tell, and laid it in other hands, she was calm and still under his handling.

'You'll need to get some rest now,' said Cadfael, 'if you've been up fretting all night, and after this blow. Whatever needs to be done Father Abbot will do. There! I'll not cover it, better to have it open to the air, but as soon as you're dismissed go home and keep from the frost. Frost can fester.' He made a leisurely business of putting away such things as he had used, to give her time to think and breathe. 'Your nephew works here with me. But of course you know that. I remember you visited him here in the garden a few days ago. A good lad, your Benet.'

After a brief, deep silence she said: 'So I have always found him.' And for the first time, though pallidly and briefly, she smiled.

'Hard-working and willing! I shall miss him if he goes, but he's worth a more testing employment.'

She said nothing to that. Her silence was marked, as though words hovered behind it ready for spilling, and were strongly held back. She said no more, barring a sedate word of thanks, when he led her back to the great court, where a buzzing murmur of voices like a disturbed hive met them before ever they rounded the hedge. Abbot Radulfus was there, and had the brothers already mustering about him, bright and quivering with curiosity, their sleepiness almost forgotten.

'We have cause to fear,' said Radulfus, wasting no words, 'that some accident has befallen Father Ailnoth. He went out from his house towards the town last night, before Compline, and no one has any word of him since. He has not been home, nor did he attend with us in church overnight. He may have suffered a fall on the ice, and lain either senseless, or unable to walk, through the night. It is my order that those of you who did not serve throughout the night in the choir should take some food quickly, and go out to search for him. The last we know of him is that he had passed our gate before Compline, hurrying towards the town. From that point we must consider and attempt every path he may have taken, for who knows upon what parish errand he was called forth? Those of you who have been wakeful all night long, take food and then sleep, and you are excused attendance from the office, so that you may be fit to take up the search when your fellows return. Robert, see to it! Brother Cadfael will show where Father Ailnoth was last seen. The searchers had best go forth in pairs or more, for two at least may be needed if he is found injured. But I pray he may be found in reasonable case, and quickly.'

Brother Cadfael intercepted a startled and solemn Benet at the edge of the dispersing crowd. The boy had a distracted look about him, between mild guilt and deep bewilderment. He jutted a dubious underlip at Cadfael, and shook his head vehemently, as if to shake off some clinging illusion that made no sense, and yet would not be ignored.

'You won't need me today. I'd best go with them.'

'No,' said Cadfael decidedly. 'You stay here and look after Mistress Hammet. Take her home if she'll go, or find her a warm corner in the gatehouse and stay with her. I know where I met with the priest, and I'll see the hunt started. If anyone wants me, you can answer for me that I'll be back as soon as may be.'

'But you've been up the better part of the night,' protested Benet, hesitating.

'And you?' said Cadfael, and made off towards the gatehouse before Benet could reply.

Ailnoth had passed by in the evening like a black arrow from a war-bow, so blind, so deaf that he had neither seen Brother Cadfael nor heard his greeting, called clearly into a brazen frost that rang like bells. At that point in the Foregate he could have been making for the bridge, in which case his urgent business was with someone in the town itself, or for any of the paths which diverged from the Foregate beyond this point. Of these there were four, one to the right, down into the riverside level of the Gaye, where the abbey's main gardens spread for almost half a mile in plots, fields and orchards, and gave place at last to woodland, and a few scattered homesteads; three to the left, a first path turning in on the near side of the mill-pond, to serve the mill and the three small houses fringing the water there, the second performing the same function for the three on the opposite side. Each of these paths was prolonged alongside the water, but to end blindly at the obstacle of the Meole Brook. The third was the narrow but well-used road that turned left just short of the Severn bridge, crossed the Meole Brook by a wooden foot-bridge where it emptied into the river, and continued south-west into woodland country leading towards the Welsh border.

And why should Father Ailnoth be hurtling like the wrath of God towards any one of these paths? The town had seemed a likelier aim, but others were taking care of enquiries there, whether the watch at the gate had seen him, whether he had stopped to enquire for anyone, whether a black, menacing shadow had passed by under the gatehouse torches. Cadfael turned his attention to the more devious ways, and halted to consider, on the very spot, so far as he could judge, where Ailnoth had passed him by.

The Foregate parish of Holy Cross embraced both sides of the road, on the right stretching well into the scattered hamlets beyond the suburb, on the left as far as the brook. Had Ailnoth been bent upon visiting someone in a country croft, he would have started directly eastward from his house in the alley opposite the abbey gatehouse, and never entered the Foregate highway at all, unless his goal was one of the few dwellings beyond the Gaye. Small ground to cover there. Cadfael deployed two parties in that direction, and turned his attention towards the west. Three paths here, one that became a regular road and would take time, two that were near, short and could surely be cleared up with little delay. And in any case, what would Ailnoth be doing at that late hour, setting out on a longer journey? No, he was on his way to some place or person close by, for what purpose only he knew.

The path on the near side of the mill-pond left the road as a decent cart track, since it had to carry the local corn to the mill, and bring the flour homeward again. It passed by the three small houses that crowded close to the highway, between their doors and the boundary wall of the abbey, reached the small plateau by the mill, where a wooden bridge crossed the head-race, and thence wandered on as a mere footpath in rough meadow grass by the edge of the water, where several pollarded willows leaned crookedly from the high bank. The first and second cottages were occupied by elderly people who had purchased bed and board for life by the grant of their own property to the abbey. The third belonged to the miller, who had been in the church throughout the night offices, to Cadfael's knowledge, and was here among the searchers now in mid morning. A devout man, as well as sedulous in preserving the favour he enjoyed with the Benedictines, and the security of his employment.

'Not a soul did I see along the waterside,' said the miller, shaking his head, 'when I came out last night to go to church, and that must have been much the same time as Brother Cadfael met with Father Ailnoth on the road. But I went straight through the wicket into the great court, not along the track, so he could have been bound this way only a matter of minutes later, for all I know. The old dame in the house next mine is house-bound once the frosts begin, she'd be home.'

'And deaf as a stone,' said Brother Ambrose flatly. 'Any man who called for help outside her door, no matter how loudly, would call in vain.'

'I meant, rather,' said the miller, 'that Father Ailnoth may have set out to visit her, knowing she dared not stir out even as far as the church. It's his duty to visit the aged and infirm,

72

for their comfort. . . .'

The face Cadfael had glimpsed in the frosty night, flaring and fading as it surged past the torches, had not looked to him as if its errand was one of comfort, but he did not say so. Even the miller, charitably advancing the possibility, had sounded dubious.

'But even if he did not,' he said, rallying stoutly, 'the maidservant who looks after the old dame has sharp enough ears, and may have heard or seen him if he did pass this way.'

They separated into two parties, to comb the paths on either side the water, Brother Ambrose taking the far side, where it was but a narrow, beaten footpath serving the three little houses and continuing along the waterside under their sloping gardens, Cadfael the cart track that led to the mill, and there dwindled into a footpath in its turn. On both the white sheen of frost was dimpled and darkened by a few footprints, but those belonged all to the morning. The rime had silvered and concealed any that might have been made by night.

The elderly couple living retired in the first house had not been out of their door since the previous day, and had heard nothing of the priest being missing. Such sensational news had them gaping in an excitement partly pleasurable, and set their tongues wagging in exclamation and lamentation, but elicited no information at all. They had shuttered their window and barred their door early, made up a steady fire, and slept undisturbed. The man, once a forester in the abbey's portion of the forest of Eyton, went in haste to pull on his boots and wrap himself in a sacking cape, and join the hunt.

At the second house the door was opened to them by a pretty slattern of about eighteen, with a mane of dark hair and bold, inquisitive eyes. The tenant was merely a high, querulous voice from the inner room, demanding why the door stood open to let in the cold. The girl whisked away for a moment to reassure her, speaking in a loud screech and perhaps with much gesture, for the complaint sank to a satisfied mumble. The girl came back to them, swathing a shawl about her and closing the door behind her to forestall further complaint.

'No,' she said, shaking her dark mane vigorously, 'not a soul that I know of came along here in the night, why should they? Never a sound did I hear after dark, and she was in her bed as soon as the daylight went, and she'd sleep through the trump of doom. But I was awake until later, and there was nothing to hear or see.'

They left her standing on the doorstone, curious and eager, gazing after them along the track as they passed the third house and came to the tall bulk of the mill. Here, with no houses in between, the still surface of the mill-pond opened on their right hand, dull silver, widening and shallowing into a round pool towards the road from which they had come, tapering gradually before them into the stream that carried the water back to the Meole Brook and the river. Rimy grass overhung the high bank, undercut here by the strength of the tail-race. And still no sign of any black form anywhere in the wintry pallor. The frost had done no more than form a thin frill of ice in the shallows, where the reed beds thickened and helped to hold it. The track reached the mill and became a narrow path, winding between the steep-roofed building and the precinct wall, and crossing the head-race by a little wooden bridge with a single hand-rail. The wheel was still, the sluice above it closed, and the overflow discharging its steady stream aside into the tail-race deep below, and so out into the pool, a silent force perceptible only as a shudder along the surface, which otherwise lay so still.

'Even if he came here,' said the miller, shaking his head, 'he would not go further. There's nothing beyond.'

No, nothing beyond but the path ambling along the grassy plain of the narrow meadow, to dwindle into nothing above the junction of brook and outflow. Fishermen came there sometimes, in season, children played there in the summer, lovers walked there in the twilight, perhaps, but who would walk that way on a frosty night? None the less, Cadfael walked on a little way. Here a few willows grew, leaning out over the water at a drunken angle by reason of the current which was gnawing under the bank. The younger ones had never yet been trimmed, but there were also two or three pollarded trunks, and one cut right down to a stump and bristling with a circle of new wands fine and springy as hairs on a giant, tonsured head. Cadfael passed by the first trees, and stood in the tufted wintry grass on the very edge of the high bank.

The motion of the tail-race, flowing out into the centre of the pool, continued its rippling path through the leaden stillness. Its influence, diminished but present, caused the faintest tremor under the bank on either side for a matter of perhaps ten paces, dying into the metallic lustre just beneath where Cadfael stood. It was that last barely perceptible shimmer that first drew his eyes down, but it was the dull fold of underlying darkness, barely stirring, that held his gaze. An edge of dark cloth, sluggishly swaying beneath the jutting grass of the bank. He went on his knees in the lingering rime, parting the grass to lean over and peer into the water. Black cloth, massed against the naked soil and the eroded willow roots, where the thrust of the tail-race had pushed it aside and tidied it out of the way, and almost out of sight. Twin pallors swayed gently, articulated like strange fish Cadfael had once seen drawn in a traveller's book. Open and empty, Father Ailnoth's hands appealed to a clearing sky, while a fold of his cloak half-covered his face.

Cadfael rose to his feet, and turned a sombre face upon his companions, who were standing by the plank bridge, gazing across the open water to where the other party was just appearing below the gardens of the townward cottages.

'He is here,' said Cadfael. 'We have found him.'

It was no small labour to get him out, even when Brother Ambrose and his fellows, hailed from their own fruitless hunt by the miller's bull's bellow and excited waving, came hurrying round from the road to lend a hand in the work.

The high, undercut bank, with deep water beneath it, made it impossible to reach down and get a hold on his clothing, even when the lankiest of them lay flat on his face and stretched long arms down, to grope still short of the surface. The miller brought a boat hook from among his store of tools, and with care they guided the obdurate body along to the edge of the tail-race, where they could descend to water level and grasp the folds of his garments.

The black, ominous bird had become an improbable fish. He lay in the grass, when they had carried him up to level ground, streaming pond-water from wiry black hair and sodden black garments, his uncovered face turned up to the chill winter light marbled blue and grey, with lips parted and eyes half-open, the muscles of cheeks and jaw and neck drawn tight with a painful suggestion of struggle and terror. A cold, cold, lonely death in the dark, and mysteriously his corpse bore the marks of it even when the combat was over. They looked down at him in awe, and no one had anything to say. What they did they did practically, without fuss, in blank silence.

They took a door from its hinges in the mill, and laid him on it, and carried him away through the wicket in the wall into the great court, and thence to the mortuary chapel. They dispersed then about their various businesses, as soon as Abbot Radulfus and Prior Robert had been apprised of their return, and what they brought with them. They were glad to go, to be off to the living, and to the festival the living were still keeping, glad to have the sanction of the season to feel happiness and have a great thing to celebrate.

The word went round the Foregate almost furtively, whispered from ear to ear, without exclaim, without many words, taking its time to reach the outer fringes of the parish, but by nightfall it was known to all. The thanksgiving made no noise, no one acknowledged it or mentioned it, no one visibly exulted. Nevertheless, the parishioners of the Foregate kept Christmas with the heartfelt fervour of a people from whom an oppressive shadow had been lifted overnight.

In the mortuary chapel, where even at this end of the year no warmth could be employed, those gathered about the bier shivered and blew into their bunched fingers wringing the rough, fingerless mittens to set the chill blood flowing and work off the numbness. Father Ailnoth, colder than them all, nevertheless lay indifferent to the gathering frost even in his nakedness, and on his bed of stone.

'We must, then, conclude,' said Abbot Radulfus heavily, 'that he fell into the pool and drowned. But why was he there at such an hour, and on the eve of the Nativity?'

There was no one prepared to answer that. To reach the place where he had been found he must have passed by every near habitation without word or sign, to end in a barren, unpeopled solitude.

'He drowned, certainly,' said Cadfael.

'Is it known,' wondered Prior Robert, 'whether he could swim?'

Cadfael shook his head. 'I've no knowledge of that, I doubt if anyone here knows. But it might not be of much importance whether he could or no. Certainly he drowned. It is less certain, I fear, that he simply fell into the water. See here – the back of his head . . .'

He raised the dead man's head with one hand, and propped head and shoulders with the right arm, and Brother Edmund, who had already viewed this corpse with him before ever Abbot Radulfus and Prior Robert were summoned, held a candle to show the nape and the thick circlet of wiry black hair. A broken wound, with edges of skin grazed loose round it and a bleached, moist middle now only faintly discoloured with blood after its soaking in the pool, began just at the rim of the tonsure, and scraped down raggedly through the circle of hair, to end where the inward curve of the nape began.

'He suffered a blow on the head here, before ever he entered the water,' said Cadfael.

'Struck from behind him,' said the abbot, with fastidious disdain, and peered closer. 'You are sure he drowned? This blow could not have killed him? For what you are saying is that this was no accident, but a deliberate assault. Or could he have come by this innocently? Is it possible? The track there is rutted, and it was icy. Could he have fallen and injured himself thus?'

'I doubt it. If a man's feet go from under him he may sit down heavily, even sprawl back on his shoulders, but he seldom goes full-length so violently as to hit his head forcibly on the ground and break his crown. That could not happen on such rough ground, only on smooth sheet ice. And mark, this is not on the round of his head, which would have taken such a shock, but lower, even moving into the curve of his neck, and lacerated, as if he was struck with something rough and jagged. And you saw the shoes he was wearing, felted beneath the sole. I think he went safer from a fall, last night, than most men.'

'Certainly, then, a blow,' said Radulfus. 'Could it have killed?'

'No, impossible! His skull is not broken. Not enough to kill, nor even to do him much lasting harm. But he might well have been stunned for a while, or so dazed that he was helpless when he fell into the water. Fell,' said Cadfael with deliberation, but ruefully, 'or was pushed in.'

'And of those two,' said the abbot with cold composure, 'which is the more likely?'

'In darkness,' said Cadfael, 'any man may step too near a sloping edge and misjudge his footing where a bank overhangs water. But whatever his reason for going along that path, why should he persist beyond the last dwelling? But this broken head I do not believe he got by any natural fall, and he got it before he went into the water. Some other hand, some other person, was there with him, and party to this death.'

'There is nothing in the wound, no fragment to show what manner of weapon it was that struck him?' ventured Brother Edmund, who had worked with Brother Cadfael in similar cases, and found good reason to require his judgement even in the minutest details. But he did not sound hopeful.

'How could there be?' said Cadfael simply. 'He has lain in the water all through the night, everything about him is bleached and sodden. If there had ever been soil or grass in his grazes, it would have soaked away long ago. But I do not think there was. He cannot alone have staggered far after that blow was struck, and he was just past the tail-race, or it would have drifted him the opposing way. Nor would anyone have carried or dragged him far if he was stunned, he being a big, heavy man, and the blow being only briefly disabling, not killing. Not ten paces from where we found him, I judge, he went into the pool. And close by that same stretch he got this blow. On top of all, there he was on grass unrutted by wheels, being past the mill – only rough and tufted, as winter turf is. If he had slipped and fallen, the ground there might have half-stunned him, but it would not have broken his head and fetched blood. I have told you all I can tell from this poor body,' he said wearily. 'Make what you can of it.'

'Murder!' said Prior Robert, rigid with indignation and horror. 'Murder is what I make of it. Father Abbot, what is now to be done?'

Radulfus brooded for some minutes over the indifferent corpse which had been Father Ailnoth, and never before so still and quiet, so tolerant of the views of others. Then he said, with measured regret: 'I am afraid, Robert, we have no choice but to inform the lord sheriff's deputy, since Hugh Beringar himself is elsewhere about his own duties.' And with his eyes still upon the livid face on the stone slab he said, with bleak wonder: 'I knew he had not made himself loved. I had not realised that in so short a time he could make himself so hated.'

Chapter Six

Young Alan Herbard, who was Hugh's deputy in his absence, came down hot-foot from the castle with the most experienced of his sergeants, William Warden, and two other officers in his train. Even if Herbard had not been well acquainted with the Foregate and its people, Will Warden certainly was, and went in no misapprehension concerning the degree of love the congregation of Holy Cross had for its new priest.

'There'll be very little mourning for him hereabouts,' he said bluntly, viewing the dead man without emotion. 'He made a thorough job of turning every soul in the parish against him. A poor end, though, for any man. A poor, cold end!'

They examined the head wound, noted the account rendered by every man who had taken part in the search, and listened to the careful opinions put forward by Brother Edmund and Brother Cadfael, and to everything Dame Diota had to say of her master's evening departure, and the anxious night she had spent worrying about his failure to return.

She had refused to depart, and waited all this time to repeat her story, which she did with a drained but steady composure, now that the matter and the mystery were out of her hands. Benet was beside her, attentive and solicitous, a very sombre Benet, with creased brows and hazel eyes clouded by something between anxiety on her account and sheer puzzlement on his own.

'If you'll give me leave,' said the boy, as soon as the

officers had withdrawn from the precinct to go in search of the provost of the Foregate, who knew his people as well as any man could, 'I'll take my aunt back to the house now, and see her settled with a good fire. She needs to rest.' And he added, appealing to Cadfael: 'I won't stay long. I may be wanted here.'

'Stay as long as is needful,' said Cadfael readily. 'I'll answer for you if there should be any questions. But what could you have to tell? I know you were in the church well before Matins began.' And knew, moreover, where the boy had been later on, and probably not alone, but he said nothing about that. 'Has anything been said about making provision for Mistress Hammet's future? This leaves her very solitary, but for you, and still almost a stranger here. But I'm sure Abbot Radulfus will see to it she's not left friendless.'

'He came himself to speak to her,' said Benet, a faint flush and gleam of his usual brightness appearing for a moment, in appreciation of such considerate usage. 'He says she need not be troubled at all, for she came here in good faith to serve the church in her proper station, and the church will see to it that she is provided for. Dwell in the house and care for it, he said, until a new priest is preferred to the benefice, and then we'll see. But in no case shall she be cast away.'

'Good! Then you and she can rest with easy minds. Terrible this may be, but it's no fault of yours or hers, and you should not brood on it.' They were both looking at him then with still, shocked faces that expressed nothing of grief or reassurance, but only stunned acceptance. 'Stay and sleep there, if you see fit,' he said to Benet. 'She may be glad of having you close by, tonight.'

Benet said neither yes nor no to that, nor did the woman. They went out silently from the ante-room of the gatehouse, where they had sat out the long uncertainty of the morning together, and crossing the wide highway of the Foregate, vanished into the narrow mouth of the alley opposite, still silvered with hoar-frost between its enclosing walls.

Cadfael felt no great surprise when Benet was back within

the hour, instead of taking advantage of the permission to absent himself overnight. He came looking for Cadfael in the garden, and found him, for once, virtually idle in his workshop, sitting by the glowing brazier. The boy sat down silently beside him, and heaved a glum sigh.

'Agreed!' said Cadfael, stirring out of his thoughts at the sound. 'We're none of us quite ourselves today, small wonder. But no need for you to rack your conscience, surely. Have you left your aunt all alone?'

'No,' said Benet. 'There's a neighbour with her, though I doubt if she's all that glad of the kind attention. There'll be more of them, I daresay, before long, bursting with curiosity and worming the whole story out of her. Not for grief, either, to judge by the one I left with her. They'll be chattering like starlings all over the parish, and never stop until night falls.'

'They'll stop fast enough, you'll find,' said Cadfael drily, 'as soon as Alan Herbard or one of his sergeants puts a word in. Let one officer show his face, and silence will fall. There's not a soul in the Foregate will own to knowing anything about anything once the questions begin.'

Benet shifted uneasily on the wooden bench, as though his bones rather than his conscience felt uncomfortable. 'I never understood that he was quite so blackly disliked. Do you truly think they'll hang together so close, and never betray even if they know who brought him to his death?'

'Yes, I do think it. For there's hardly a soul but will feel it might as easily have been his own act, but for God's grace. But it need not fret you, one way or the other. Unless it was you who broke his head?' said Cadfael mildly. 'Was it?'

'No,' said Benet as simply, staring down into his linked hands; and the next moment looked up with sharp curiosity: 'But what makes *you* so sure of it?'

'Well, firstly, I saw you in church well before it was time for Matins, and though there's no certainty just when Ailnoth went into the pool, I should judge it was probably after that time. Secondly, I know of no reason why you

82

should bear him any grudge, and you said yourself it comes as a surprise to you he was so hated. But thirdly and best, from what I know of you, lad, if you took such dire offence as to up and hit a man, it would not be from behind, but face to face.'

'Well, thank you for that!' said Benet, briefly recovering his blazing smile. 'But, Cadfael, what *do* you think happened? It was you saw him last, alive, at least as far as is known. Was there any other soul about there? Did you see anyone else? Anyone, as it might be, following him?'

'Never a creature beyond the gatehouse here. There were folk from the Foregate just coming in for the service, but none going on towards the town. Any others who may have seen Ailnoth can only have seen him before ever I did, and with nothing to show where he was bound. Unless someone had speech with him. But by the way he went scurrying past me, I doubt if he halted for any other.'

Benet considered that in silence for a long moment, and then said, rather to himself than to Cadfael: 'And from his house it's so short a way. He'd come into the Foregate just opposite the gatehouse. Small chance of being seen or stopped in that distance.'

'Leave it to the King's officers to scratch their heads over the how and why,' Cadfael advised. 'They'll find no lack of folk who'll pretend no sorrow at seeing the last of Ailnoth, but I doubt if they'll get much information out of anyone, man, woman or child. No blinking it, the man generated grudges wherever he stepped. He may well have made the most perfect of clerks, where he had to deal only with documents, charters and accounts, but he had no notion how to coax and counsel and comfort common human sinners. And what else is a parish priest for?'

The frost continued that night, harder than ever, freezing over the reedy shallows in the mill-pond, and fringing the townward shore with a white shelf of ice, but not yet sealing over the deeper water or the tremulous path of the tail-race, so that the little boys who went hopefully to examine the ice in the early morning returned disappointed. No point as yet in trying to break the iron ground for Father Ailnoth's grave, even if Herbard would have permitted an early burial, but at least the clear cold made delay acceptable.

In the Foregate a kind of breathless hush brooded. People talked much but in low voices and only among trusted friends, and yet everywhere there was a feeling of suppressed and superstitious gladness, as if a great cloud had been lifted from the parish. Even those who did not confide in one another in words did so in silent glances. The relief was everywhere, and palpable.

But so was the fear. For someone, it seemed, had rid the Foregate of its blight, and all those who had wished it away felt a morsel of the guilt sticking to their fingers. They could not but speculate on the identity of their deliverer, even while they shut their mouths and their eyes, and put away all knowledge of their own suspicions, for fear of betraying them to the law.

All through the routine of the day Cadfael pursued his own thoughts, and they centred, inevitably, on Ailnoth's death. No one would tell Alan Herbard about Eadwin's headland or Aelgar's grievance, or the unconsecrated grave of Centwin's son, or any of the dozen or more other wounds that had made Ailnoth a hated man, but there would be no need. Will Warden would know them all already, and maybe other, lesser offences of which even the abbot had not been told. Every one of those thus aggrieved would be examined as to his movements on the eve of the Nativity, and Will would know where to look for confirmation. And much as the Foregate might sympathise with whoever had killed Ailnoth, and loyally as they would close round him and cover him, it was nevertheless vital that the truth should be known, for there would be no real peace of mind for anyone until it was discovered. That was the first reason why Cadfael, almost against his will, wished for a solution. The second was for the sake of Abbot Radulfus, who carried, in his own mind, a double guilt, for bringing to the fold so ill-fitted a shepherd, and for suffering him to be done to death by some enraged ram among the flock. Bitter though it may be to many, Cadfael concluded, there is no substitute for truth, in this or any case.

Meantime, in occasional reversions to the day's labours, he was thankful that Benet had completed the winter digging just in time, before the hard frost came, and attacked the final thin crop of weeds in all the flower beds so vigorously that now the earth could sleep snugly under the rime, and the whole enclosed garden looked neat and clean, and content as a hedge-pig curled up an arm's length down under leaves and grass and dry herbage until the spring.

A good worker, the boy Benet, cheerful and ungrudging, and good company. Somewhat clouded by the death of this man who had brought him here, and at least never done him any harm, but his natural buoyancy would keep breaking through. Not much was left, now, of the candidate for the cloister. Had that been the one sign of human frailty in Father Ailnoth, that he had deliberately represented his groom on the journey north as desirous of the monastic life, though still a little hesitant to take the final step? A lie to get the boy off his hands? Benet was firm that he had never given voice to any such wish, and Benet, in Cadfael's considered opinion, would make a very poor liar. Come to think of it, not very much left, either, of the wide-eyed, innocent, unlettered bumpkin Benet had first affected, at least not here in the solitude of the garden. He could still slip it on like a glove if for any reason the prior accosted him. Either he thinks me blind, said Cadfael to himself, or he does not care at all to pretend with me. And I am very sure he does not think me blind!

Well, a day or two more, and surely Hugh would be back. As soon as he was released from attendance on the King he would be making his way home by forced marches. Aline and Giles between them would take care of that. God send he would come home with the right answer!

And it seemed that Hugh had indeed made all haste to get home to his wife and son, for he rode into Shrewsbury late in the evening of the twenty-seventh, to hear from a relieved Alan Herbard of the turmoil that awaited solution, the death that came rather as blessing than disaster to the people of the Foregate, but must none the less be taken very seriously by the King's officers. He came down immediately after Prime next morning, to get the most authoritative account from the abbot, and confer with him over the whole troublesome matter of the priest's relationship with his flock. He had also another grave matter of his own to confide.

Cadfael knew nothing of Hugh's return until mid morning, when his friend sought him out in the workshop. The broken-glass grating of boots on the frozen gravel made Cadfael turn from his mortar, knowing the step but hardly believing in it.

'Well, well!' he said, delighted. 'I hadn't thought to clap eyes on you for a day or two yet. Glad I am to see you, and I hope I read the signs aright?' He broke free from Hugh's embrace to hold him off at arm's length and study his face anxiously. 'Yes, you have the look of success about you. Do I see you confirmed in office?'

'You do, old friend, you do! And kicked out promptly to my shire to be about my master's business. Trust me, Cadfael, he's come back to us lean and hungry and with the iron-marks on him, and he wants action, and vengeance, and blood. If he could but keep up this fury of energy, he could finish this contention within the year. But it won't last,' said Hugh philosophically, 'it never does. God, but I'm still stiff with all the riding I've done. Have you got a cup of wine about you, and half an hour to sit and waste with me?'

He flung himself down gratefully on the wooden bench and stretched out his feet to the warmth of the brazier, and Cadfael brought cups and a flagon, and sat down beside him, taking pleasure in viewing the slight figure and thin, eloquent face that brought in with them the whole savour of the outside world, fresh from the court, ratified in office, a man whose energy did not flag as Stephen's did, who did not abandon one enterprise to go off after another, as Stephen did. Or were those days now over? Perhaps the King's privations and grievances in prison in Bristol had put an end to all half-hearted proceedings in the future. But plainly Hugh did not think him capable of sustaining so great a change.

'He wore his crown again at the Christmas feast, and a sumptuous affair it was. Give him his due, there's no man living could look more of a king than Stephen. He questioned me closely in private as to how things shape in these parts, and I gave him a full account of how we stand with the earl of Chester, and the solid ally Owain Gwynedd has been to us there in the north of the shire. He seemed content enough with me – at least he clouted me hard on the back – a fist like a shovel, Cadfael! – and gave me his authority to get on with the work as sheriff confirmed. He even recalled how I ever came to get his countenance as Prestcote's deputy. I fancy that's a rare touch in kings, part of the reason why we cling to Stephen even when he maddens us. So I got not only his sanction, but a great shove to get back on the road and back to my duty. I think he means to make a visit north when the worst of the winter's over, to buckle a few more of the waverers to him again. Lucky I'd thought to get a change of horses four times on the way south,' said Hugh thankfully, 'thinking I might be in haste coming back. I'd left my grey in Oxford, going down. And here I am, glad to be home.'

'And Alan Herbard will be glad to see you home,' said Cadfael, 'for he's been dropped into deep water while you've been away. Not that he shrinks from it, though he can hardly have welcomed it. He'll have told you what's happened here? On the very Nativity! A bad business!'

'He's told me. I've just come from the abbot, to get his

view of it. I saw but little of the man, but I've heard enough from others. A man well hated, and in so short a time. Is their view of him justified? I could hardly ask Abbot Radulfus to cry his candidate down, but I would not say he had any great regard for him.'

'A man without charity or humility,' said Cadfael simply. 'Salted with those, he might have been a decent fellow, but both were left out of him. He came down over the parish like a cloud of blight, suddenly.'

'And you're sure it was murder? I've seen his body, I know of the head wound. Hard to see, I grant you, how he could have come by that by accident, or alone.'

'You'll have to pursue it,' said Cadfael, 'whatever poor angry soul struck the blow. But you'll get no help from the Foregate folk. Their hearts will be with whoever rid them of the shadow.'

'So Alan says, too,' said Hugh, briefly smiling. 'He knows these people pretty shrewdly, young as he is. And he'd rather I should harry them than he. And inasmuch as I must, I will. I'm warned off charity and humility myself,' said Hugh ruefully, 'on the King's affairs. He wants his enemies hunted down without remorse, and is giving orders right and left to that effect. And I have a charge to be the hunter here in my shire, for one of them.'

'Once before, as I recall,' said Cadfael, refilling his friend's cup, 'he gave you a task to do that you did in your own way, which certainly was not his when he gave the order. He never questioned your way, after. He may as well repent of this, later, and be glad if you shuffle your feet somewhat in the hunt. Not that I need to tell you as much, since you know it all before.'

'I can make a goodly show,' agreed Hugh, grinning, 'and still bear in mind that he might not be grateful for overmuch zeal, once he gets over his grudges. I never knew him bear malice for long. He did his worst here in Shrewsbury, and dislikes to be reminded of it now. The thing is this, Cadfael. Back in the summer, when it seemed the Empress had crown and sceptre and all in her hands, FitzAlan in Normandy is known to have sent over a couple of scouts of his following, to sound out the extent of her support, and see if the time was ripe to bring a fresh force over to add to her strength. How they were discovered I haven't heard, but when her fortunes were reversed, and the Queen brought her army up into London and beyond, these two venturers were cut off from return, and have been one leap ahead of capture ever since. One of them is thought to have got off successfully from Dunwich, but the other is still loose somewhere, and since he's been hunted without result in the south, the cry is now that he's made his way north to get out of range, and try to make contact with sympathisers of Anjou for help. So all the King's sheriffs are ordered to keep a strict watch for him. After his rough treatment, Stephen's in no mind to forgive and forget. I'm obliged to make a show of zeal, and that means making the matter public by proclamation, and so I shall. For my part, I'm glad to know that one of them has slipped overseas again safely, back to his wife. Nor would I be sorry if I heard that the second had followed him. Two bold boys venturing over here alone, putting their skins at risk for a cause – why should I have anything against them? Nor will Stephen, when he comes to himself.'

'You use very exact terms,' said Cadfael curiously. 'How do you know they are mere boys? And how do you know that the one who's fled back to Normandy has a wife?'

'Because, my Cadfael, it's known who they are, the pair of them, youngsters very close to FitzAlan. The hart we're still hunting is one Ninian Bachiler. And the lad who's escaped us, happily, is a certain young fellow named Torold Blund, whom both you and I have good cause to remember.' He laughed, seeing how Cadfael's face brightened in astonished pleasure. 'Yes, the same long lad you hid in the old mill along the Gaye, some years back. And now reported as son-in-law to FitzAlan's closest friend and ally, Fulke Adeney. Yes, Godith got her way!'

Good cause to remember, indeed! Cadfael sat warmed

through by the recollection of Godith Adeney, for a short time his garden boy Godric to the outer world, and the young man she had helped him to succour and send away safely into Wales. Man and wife now, it seemed. Yes, Godith had got her way!

'To think,' said Hugh, 'that I might have married her! If my father had lived longer, if I'd never come to Shrewsbury to put my newly inherited manors at Stephen's disposal, and never set eyes on Aline, I might well have married Godith. No regrets, I fancy, on either side. She got a good lad, and I got Aline.'

'And you're sure he's slipped away safely out of England, back to her?'

'So it's reported. And so may his fellow slip away, with my goodwill,' said Hugh heartily, 'if he's Torold's match, and can oblige me by keeping well out of my way. Should you happen on him, Cadfael – you have a way of happening on the unexpected – keep him out of sight. I'm in no mind to clap a good lad into prison for being loyal to a cause which isn't mine.'

'You have a good excuse for setting his case aside,' Cadfael suggested thoughtfully, 'seeing you're come home to find a slain man on the doorstep, and a priest at that.'

'True, I could argue that as the prior case,' agreed Hugh, setting his empty cup aside and rising to take his leave. 'All the more as this affair is indeed laid right at my door, and for all I know young Bachiler may be a hundred miles away or more. A small show of zeal, however, won't come amiss, or do any harm.'

Cadfael went out into the garden with him. Benet was just coming up over the far rim of the rose garden, where the ground sloped away to the pease fields and the brook. He was whistling jauntily as he came, and swinging an axe lightly in one hand, for a little earlier he had been breaking the ice on the fish ponds, to let air through to the denizens below.

'What did you say, Hugh, was the christened name of this

young man Bachiler you're supposed to be hunting?'
'Ninian, or so he's reported.'
'Ah, yes!' said Cadfael. 'That was it – Ninian.'

Benet came back into the garden after his dinner with the lay servants, and looked about him somewhat doubtfully, kicking at the hard-frozen ground he had recently dug, and viewing the clipped hedges now silvered with rime that lasted day-long and increased by a fresh frilling of white every night. Every branch that stirred tinkled like glass. Every clod was solid as stone.

'What is there for me to do?' he demanded, tramping into Cadfael's workshop. 'This frost halts everything. No man could plough or dig, a day like this. Let alone copy letters,' he added, round eyed at the thought of the numb fingers in the scriptorium trying to line in a capital with precious gold-leaf, or even write an unshaken line. 'They're still at it, poor wretches. At least there's some warmth in handling a spade or an axe. Can I split you some wood for the brazier? Lucky for us you need the fire for your brews, or we should be as blue and stiff as the scribes.'

'They'll have lighted the fire in the warming room early, a day like this,' said Cadfael placidly, 'and when they can no longer hold pen or brush steady they have leave to stop work. You've done all the digging within the walls here, and the pruning's finished, no need to feel guilty if you sit idle for once. Or you can take a turn at these mysteries of mine if you care to. Nothing learned is ever quite wasted.'

Benet was ready enough to try his hand at anything. He came close, to peer curiously at what Cadfael was stirring in a stone pot on a grid on the side of the brazier. Here in their shared solitude he was quite easy, and had lost the passing disquiet and dismay that had dimmed his brightness on Christmas Day. Men die, and thinking men see a morsel of their own death in every one that draws close to them, but the young soon recover. And what was Father Ailnoth to Benet, after all? If he had done him a kindness in letting him come here with his aunt, the priest had none the less had the benefit of the boy's willing service on the journey, a fair exchange.

'Did you visit Mistress Hammet last evening?' asked Cadfael, recalling another possible source of concern. 'How is she now?'

'Still bruised and shaken,' said Benet, 'but she has a stout spirit, she'll do well enough.'

'She hasn't been greatly worried by the sergeants? Hugh Beringar is home now, and he'll want to hear everything from her own lips, but she need not trouble for that. Hugh has been told how it was, she need only repeat it to him.'

'They've been civility itself with her,' said Benet. 'What is this you're making?'

It was a large pot, and a goodly quantity of aromatic brown syrup bubbling gently in it. 'A mixture for coughs and colds,' said Cadfael. 'We shall be needing it any day now, and plenty of it, too.'

'What goes into it?'

'A great many things. Bay and mint, coltsfoot, hore-hound, mullein, mustard, poppy – good for the throat and the chest – and a small draught of the strong liquor I distil does no harm in such cases, either. But if you want work, here, lift out that big mortar . . . yes, there! Those frost-gnawed hands you were pitying, we'll make something for those.'

The chilblains of winter were always a seasonal enemy, and an extra batch of ointment for treating them could not come amiss. He began to issue orders briskly, pointing out the herbs he wanted, making Benet climb for some, and move hastily up and down the hanging bunches for others. The boy took pleasure in this novel entertainment, and jumped to obey every crisp command.

'The small scale, there, at the back of the shelf – fetch that out, and while you're in the corner there, the little weights are in the box beside. Oh, and, Ninian . . .' said Cadfael, sweet and calm and guileless as ever.

The boy, interested and off his guard, halted and swung about in response to his name, waiting with a willing smile to hear what next he should bring. And on the instant he froze where he stood, the serene brightness still visible on a face turned to marble, the smile fixed and empty. For a long moment they contemplated each other eye to eye, Cadfael also smiling, then warm blood flushed into Benet's face and he stirred out of his stillness, and the smile, wary as it was, became live and young again. The silence endured longer, but it was the boy who broke it at last.

'Now what should happen? Am I supposed to overturn the brazier, set the hut on fire, rush out and bar the door on you, and run for my life?'

'Hardly,' said Cadfael, 'unless that's what you want. It would scarcely suit me. It would become you better to put that scale down on the level slab there, and pay attention to what you and I are about. And while you're at it, that jar by the shutter is hog's fat, bring that out, too.'

Benet did so, with admirable calm now, and turned a wryly smiling face. 'How did you know? How did you know even my name?' He was making no further pretence at secrecy, he had even relaxed into a measure of perverse enjoyment.

'Son, the story of your invasion of this realm, along with another mad-head as reckless as yourself, seems to be common currency by this time, and the whole land knows you are supposed to have fled northwards from regions where you were far too hotly hunted for comfort. Hugh Beringar got his orders to keep an eye open for you, at the feast in Canterbury. King Stephen's blood is up, and until it cools your liberty is not worth a penny if his officers catch up with you. For I take it,' he said mildly, 'that you *are* Ninian Bachiler?'

'I am. But how did you know?'

'Why, once I heard that there was a certain Ninian lost somewhere in these midland counties, it was not so hard. Once you all but told me yourself. "What's your name?" I asked you, and you began to say "Ninian", and then caught yourself up and changed it to a clownish echo of the question, before you got out "Benet". And oh, my child, how soon you gave over pretending with me that you were a simple country groom. Never had a spade in your hand before! No, I swear you never had, though I grant you you learn very quickly. And your speech, and your hands — No, never blush or look mortified, it was not so obvious, it simply added together grain by grain. And besides, you stopped counting me as someone to be deceived. You may as well admit it.'

'It seemed unworthy,' said the boy, and scowled briefly at the beaten earth floor. 'Or useless, perhaps! I don't know! What are you going to do with me now? If you try to give me up, I warn you I'll do all I can to break away. But I won't do it by laying hand on you. We've been friendly together.'

'As well for both you and me,' said Cadfael, smiling, 'for you might find you'd met your match. And who said I had any notion of giving you up? I am neither King Stephen's partisan nor the Empress Maud's, and whoever serves either of them honestly and at risk to himself may go about his business freely for me. But you may as well tell me what that business is. Without implicating any other, of course. I take it, for instance, that Mistress Hammet is not your aunt?'

'No,' said Ninian slowly, his eyes intent and earnest on Cadfael's face. 'You will respect her part in this? She was in my mother's service before she married the bishop's groom. She was my nurse when I was a child. When I was in flight I went to her for help. It was thoughtless, and I wish it could be undone, but believe it, whatever she has done has been done in pure affection for me, and what I've been about is nothing to do with her. She got me these clothes I wear – mine had been living rough in the woods and in and out of rivers, but they still marked me for what I am. And it was of her own will that she asked leave to bring me here with her as her nephew, when Father Ailnoth got this preferment. To get me away from the hunters. She had asked and been given

94

his leave before ever I knew of it, I could not avoid. And it did come as a blessing to me, I own it.'

'What was your intent when you came over from Normandy?' asked Cadfael.

'Why, to make contact with any friends of the Empress who might be lying very low in the south and east, where she's least loved, and urge them to be ready to rise if FitzAlan should think the time ripe for a return. It looked well for her chances then. But when the wind changed, someone – God knows which of those we'd spoken with – took fright and covered himself by betraying us. You know we were two?'

'I know it,' said Cadfael. 'Indeed I know the second. He was of FitzAlan's household here in Shrewsbury before the town fell to the King. He got off safely from an eastern port, as I heard. You were not so lucky.'

'Is Torold clean away? Oh, you do me good!' cried Ninian, flushed with joy. 'We were separated when they almost cornered us near Bury. I feared for him! Oh, if he's safe home . . .' He caught himself up there, wincing at the thought of calling Normandy home. 'For myself, I can deal! Even if I do end in the King's prison – but I won't! Fending for one is not so hard as fretting for two. And Torold's a married man!'

'And the word is, he's gone, back to his wife. And what,' wondered Cadfael, 'is your intention now? Plainly the one you came with is a lost cause. What now?'

'Now,' said the boy with emphatic gravity, 'I mean to get across the border into Wales, and make my way down to join the Empress's army at Gloucester. I can't bring her FitzAlan's army, but I can bring her one able-bodied man to fight for her – and not a bad hand with sword or lance, though I do say it myself.'

By the lift of his voice and the sparkle in his eyes he meant it ardently, and it was a course much more congenial to him than acting as agent to reluctant allies. And why should he not succeed? The Welsh border was not so far, though the journey to Gloucester through the ill-disciplined wilds of

Powys might be long and perilous. Cadfael considered his companion thoughtfully, and beheld a young man somewhat lightly clad for winter travelling afoot, without weapons, without a horse, without wealth to grease his journeying. None of which considerations appeared to discourage Ninian.

'An honest enough purpose,' said Cadfael, 'and I see nothing against it. We have a few adherents of your faction even in these parts, though they keep very quiet these days. Could not one of them be of use to you now?'

The bait was not taken. The boy closed his lips firmly, and stared Cadfael out with impregnable composure. If he had indeed attempted to contact one of the Empress's partisans here, he was never going to admit it. With his own confidences he might favour his too perceptive mentor, but he was not going to implicate any other man.

'Well,' said Cadfael comfortably, 'it seems that you are not being hunted here with any great zeal, and your position with us is well established, no reason why Benet should not continue to do his work here quietly and modestly, and never be noticed. And if this iron frost goes on as it's begun, your work will be here among the medicines, so we may as well go on with your lesson. Look lively, now, and pay attention to what I show you.'

The boy burst into a soft, half-smothered peal of laughter in sheer relief and pleasure, like a child, and bounded to Cadfael's elbow at the mortar like a hound puppy excited by a fresh scent.

'Good, then tell me what to do, and I'll do it. I'll be half an apothecary before I leave you. Nothing learned,' said Ninian, with an impudently accurate imitation of Cadfael's more didactic style, 'is ever quite wasted.'

'True, true!' agreed Cadfael sententiously. 'Nothing observed, either. You never know where it may fit into a larger vision.'

Exactly as certain details were beginning to fit together and elaborate for him the picture he had of this venturesome, light-hearted, likeable young man. A destitute young man, urgently in need of the means to make his way undetected to Gloucester, one who had come to England, no doubt, with a memorised list of names that should prove sympathetic to the Empress's cause, a few of them even here in Shropshire. A devoted woman all anxiety for her nurseling, bringing honey cakes and carrying away a small token thing that slipped easily into the breast of her gown, from the breast of Benet's cotte. And shortly thereafter, the lady Sanan Bernières, daughter of a father dispossessed for his adherence to Maud, and step-daughter to another lord of the same party, paying a brief visit from Giffard's house near Saint Chad's to buy herbs for her Christmas kitchen, and pausing in the garden to speak to the labouring boy, and look him up and down, as though, as the boy himself had reported, she were in need of a page, 'and thought I might do, given a little polishing'.

Well, well! So far everything in harmony. But why, then, was the boy still here at all, if aid had been asked and given?

Upon this incomplete picture the sudden death of Father Ailnoth intruded like a black blot in a half-written page, complicating everything, relating, apparently, to nothing, a bird of as ill omen dead as alive.

Chapter Seven

The hunt for Ninian Bachiler, as a proscribed agent of the Empress Maud at large in Stephen's territory, was duly proclaimed in Shrewsbury, and the word went round in voluble gossip, all the more exuberantly as a relief from the former sensation of Ailnoth's death, concerning which no one in the Foregate had been voluble, unless in privacy. It was good to have a topic of conversation which departed at so marked a tangent from what really preoccupied the parishioners of Holy Cross. Since none of the gossips cared a pin how many dissident agents were at large in the county, none of the talk was any threat to the fugitive, much less to Mistress Hammet's dutiful nephew Benet, who came and went freely between abbey and parsonage.

In the afternoon of the twenty-ninth of December, Cadfael was called out to the first sufferers from coughs and colds in the Foregate, and extended his visits to one elderly merchant in the town itself, a regular chest patient of his in the winter. He had left Ninian sawing and splitting wood from the pruning of the trees, and keeping cautious watch on a pot of herbs in oil of almonds, which had to warm on the edge of the brazier without simmering, to make a lotion for the frost-nipped hands too tender to endure the hog's fat base of the ointment. The boy could be trusted to abide by his instructions, and whatever he did he did with his might.

Cadfael's errands had taken him rather less time than he had expected, and the weather was not such as to encourage him to linger. He re-entered at the gatehouse with more than an hour still in hand before Vespers, and made his way across the great court and out into the garden, rounding the box hedge into the alley that led to his herbarium. In the frost he had wrapped woollen cloths about his boots to give him a grip on the icy roads, and the same sensible precaution made his steps silent on the path. So it happened that he heard the voices before he himself was heard, rapid and soft and vehement from within his workshop. And one of the voices was Ninian's, a tone above its usual pitch by reason of some fierce but subdued excitement. And the other was a girl's, insistent and agitated. Curious that she, too, should convey this same foolhardy sense of enjoyment in the experience of danger and dread. A good match! And what other girl had had to do with this place and this youth, but Sanan Bernières?

'Oh, but he would!' she was saying emphatically. 'He's there by now, he'll tell them everything, where to find you, how you sent to him – all! You must come now, quickly, before they come to take you.'

'Impossible by the gatehouse,' said Ninian, 'we should run into their arms. But I can't believe – why should he betray me? Surely he knows I'd never mention his name?'

'He's been in dread,' said the girl impatiently, 'ever since your message came, but now you're cried publicly as a wanted man, he'll do anything to shake off his own danger. He's not evil – he does as other men do, protects his own life and lands, and his son's, too – he lost enough before. . . .'

'So he did,' said Ninian, penitent. 'I never should have drawn him in. Wait, I must lift this aside, I can't leave it to boil. Cadfael. . . .'

The shameless listener, who at least had heard one motion of consideration towards him and his art, in that last utterance, suddenly came to his senses, and to the awareness that in a matter of seconds these two would be issuing forth from the hut and taking to flight, by whatever road this resourceful girl had devised. Just as soon as Ninian had lifted the soothing oil from the heat and laid it carefully in a secure spot. Bless the boy, he deserved to reach Gloucester in safety! Cadfael made haste to dart round behind the barrier of the box hedge, and freeze into stillness there. He had not time to withdraw completely, but it is not certain, in any case, that he would have done so.

They burst out of the workshop hand in hand, she leading, for she knew by what route she had entered here unobserved. Through the garden she drew him, over the rim of the slope, and down towards the Meole Brook. A dark little figure swathed in a cloak, she vanished first, dwindling rapidly out of sight down the field; Ninian followed. They were gone, along the edge of the newly ploughed and manured pease fields and out of sight. So the brook was frozen over, and so must the mill-pond be. That way she had come, straight to where she knew he would be. Yet she might, just as easily, have found Cadfael there as well. Which meant, surely, that she had had converse with Ninian since he had confided in Cadfael, and saw no reason to fear the encounter, when the need was great.

Well, they were gone. No sound came up from the hollow of the brook, and there were trees quite close on the further side for cover, and all they had to do after that was wait for the right moment, cross the brook again by the bridge that carried the westward road, and make their way discreetly to whatever hiding place she had devised for her hostage, whether in the town or out of it. If out of it, surely to the west, since that was the way he desired, at last, to go. But would Ninian consent to depart until he knew that Dame Diota was safe and suspect of nothing in connection with his own expedition? If his cover was stripped from him, then she was also exposed to question. He would not leave her so. Cadfael had begun to know this young man well enough to be certain of that.

It had grown profoundly quiet, as if the very air waited for the next and inevitable alarm. Cadfael spared a moment to peer into his workshop, saw his pot of oil placed carefully on the stone cooling slab close to the brazier, and withdrew again in some haste to the great court, and across it into the cloister, but hovering anxiously where he could watch for any invasion at the gatehouse, without himself being immediately observed.

They were longer in coming than he had expected, and for that he was grateful. Moreover, a sudden flurry of fine snow had begun to fall, and that would soon cover up the footsteps crossing the brook, and in the rising wind of evening even disguise any tracks left in the garden. Until this moment he had not had time to consider the implications of what he had overheard. Clearly Ninian's appeal had gone to Ralph Giffard, who had turned a deaf ear, all too conscious of his own danger if he responded. But the girl, born into another family no less devoted to the Empress's cause, had taken up the charge and made it her own. And now, affrighted by the public crying of an enemy spy, Giffard had thought it best to ensure his own position by carrying the whole story to Hugh Beringar. Who would not be grateful for the attention, but would be forced to act upon it, or at least to put up a fair show of doing so.

All of which left one curious point at issue: Where had Ralph Giffard been going in such purposeful haste on Christmas Eve, striding across the bridge towards the Foregate almost as impetuously as Father Ailnoth had been hastening in the opposite direction an hour or so later? The two intent figures began to look like mirror images of the same man. Giffard, perhaps, the more afraid, Ailnoth the more malevolent. There was a link somewhere there, though the join was missing.

And here they came, in at the gatehouse arch, all of them on foot, Hugh with Ralph Giffard hard and erect at his elbow, Will Warden and a couple of young officers in arms following. No need here for mounted men, they were in search of a youngster horseless and penniless, labouring in the abbey gardens, and the prison that waited for him was only walking distance away.

Cadfael took his time about appearing. Others were there first, and so much the better. Brother Jerome did not love the cold, but kept a watchful eye on the outer world whenever he hopped into the warming room on such frosty days, ready to appear at any moment, dutiful and devout. Moreover, he always knew where to find Prior Robert at need. By the time Cadfael emerged innocently from the cloister they were both there, confronting the visitors from the secular world, and a few other brethren had noted the gathering, and halted within earshot in pure human curiosity, forgetting their chilled hands and feet.

'The boy Benet?' Prior Robert was saying in tones of astonishment and disdain as Cadfael approached. 'Father Ailnoth's groom? The good father himself asked employment for this young man. What absurdity is this? The boy is scarcely better than a simpleton, a mere country lad! I have often spoken with him, I know him for an innocent. My lord sheriff, I fear this gentleman wastes your time in a mistake. This cannot be true.'

'Father Prior, by your leave,' Ralph Giffard spoke up firmly, 'it is only too true, the fellow is not what he seems. I received a message, written in a fair hand, from this same simpleton, sealed with the seal of the traitor and outlaw FitzAlan, the Empress's man who is now in France, and asking me for help in FitzAlan's name – an appeal I rightly left unanswered. I have kept the leaf, the lord sheriff has seen it for himself. He was here, he said, come with the new priest, and he needed help, news and a horse, and laid claim to my aid to get what he wanted. He begged me to meet him at the mill an hour short of midnight on Christmas Eve, when all good folk would be making ready for church. I did not go, I would not touch such treason against our lord the King. But the proof I've given to the sheriff here, and there is not nor cannot be any mistake. Your labourer Benet is FitzAlan's agent Ninian Bachiler, for so he signed himself with his own hand.'

'I fear it's true enough, Father Prior,' said Hugh briskly. 'There are questions to be asked later, but now I must ask your leave at once to seek out this Benet, and he must answer for himself. There need be no disturbance for the brothers, I am asking access only to the garden.'

It was at this point that Cadfael ambled forward out of the cloister, secure across the glazed cobbles, since his feet were still swathed in wool. He came with ears benignly pricked and countenance open as the air. The snow was still falling, in an idle, neglectful fashion, but every flake froze where it fell.

'Benet?' said Cadfael guilelessly. 'You're looking for my labouring boy? I left him not a quarter of an hour since in my workshop. What do you want with him?'

He went with them, all concern and astonishment, as they proceeded into the garden, and threw open the workshop door upon the soft glow of the brazier, the pot of herbal oil drawn close on its stone slab, and the aromatic emptiness, and from that went on to quarter the whole of the garden and the fields down to the brook, where the helpful snow had obliterated every footprint. He was as mystified as the best of them. And if Hugh avoided giving him a single sidelong look, that did not mean he had not observed every facet of this vain pursuit, rather that he had, and was in little doubt as to the purveyor of mystification. There was usually a reason for Brother Cadfael's willing non-cooperation. Moreover, there were other points to be pursued before the search was taken further.

'You tell me,' said Hugh, turning to Giffard, 'that you received this appeal for your help a day or so before Christmas Eve, when a meeting at the mill was requested, somewhat before midnight. Why did you not pass it on at once to my deputy? Something might have been done about it then. Plainly he had wind of us now, since he's fled.'

If Giffard was uneasy at this dereliction of a loyal subject's duty, he gave no sign of it, but stared Hugh fully and firmly in the face. 'Because he was merely your deputy, my lord. Had you been here. . . . You got your office first after the siege of Shrewsbury, you know how we who had taken the oath to the Empress fared then, you know of my losses.

Since then I have submitted to King Stephen, and held by my submission faithfully. But a young man like Herbard, new here, left in charge and liable to stand on his dignity and status – one ignorant of the past, and what it cost me . . . I was afraid of being held still as one attainted, even if I told honestly all that I knew. And recollect, we had then heard nothing about this Bachiler being hunted in the south, the name meant nothing to me. I thought him probably of no importance, and with no prospect of any success in whipping up support for a lost cause. So I held my peace, in spite of FitzAlan's seal. There were several of his knights held such seals in his name. Do me justice, as soon as you made public the hue and cry, and I understood what was afoot, I came to you and told you the truth.'

'I grant you did,' said Hugh, 'and I understand your doubts, though it's no part of my office to hound any man for what's past and done.'

'But now, my lord . . .' Giffard had more to say, and had plainly taken great encouragement from his own eloquence and Hugh's acquiescence, for he had burned into sudden hopeful fervour. 'Now I see more in this than either you or I have thought. For I have not quite told you all, there has hardly been time to think of everything. For see, it was this young man who came here under the protection of Father Ailnoth, vilely deceiving the priest in the pretence that he was a harmless youth seeking work, and kin to the woman who kept the priest's household. And is not Father Ailnoth, who brought him here in all innocence, now done to death and waiting for burial? Who is more likely to stand guilty of his murder than the man who took wicked advantage of his goodness, and made him an unwitting accomplice in treason?'

He knew very well what manner of bolt he was hurling into the circle of listeners, he had even drawn back a pace or two to observe the shock and to distance himself from it. There was no length to which he would not go, now, to prove his own loyal integrity, to keep what he still had, if he must eternally grudge and lament what he had lost by his former allegiance. Perhaps he was secretly relieved that the boy he traduced was well away, and need never answer, but what most troubled him was his own inviolability.

'You're accusing him of the priest's murder?' said Hugh, eyeing him narrowly. 'That's going far. On what grounds do you make such a charge?'

'The very fact that he is fled points to him.'

'That might be valid enough, but not – mark me! – not unless the priest had got wind of the deception practised on him. To the best we know there was no quarrel between them, nothing had arisen to set them at odds. Unless the priest had found out how he had been abused, there could be no ground for any hostility between them.'

'He did know,' said Giffard.

'Go on,' said Hugh after a brief, profound silence. 'You cannot stop there. How do you know the priest had found him out?'

'For the best reason. I told him! I said there was still more that I had not yet told you. On the eve of the Nativity I came down here to his house, and told him how he was cheated and abused by one he had helped. I had given it anxious thought, and though I did not go to your deputy, I felt it only right to warn Father Ailnoth how he had harboured an enemy unawares. Those of the Empress's party are threatened with excommunication now, as you, my lord sheriff, are witness. The priest had been shamefully imposed upon, and so I told him.'

So that was the way of it! That was where he had been bound in such determined haste before Compline. And that was why Father Ailnoth had rushed away vengefully to keep the nocturnal tryst and confront in person the youth who had imposed upon him. Give him his due, he was no coward, he would not run first to the sergeants and get a bodyguard, he would storm forth by the mill-pool to challenge his opponent face to face, denounce, possibly even attempt to overpower him with his own hands, certainly cry him outlaw to the abbot and to the castle if he could not himself hale him to judgement. But things had gone very differently, for Ninian had come unharmed to church, and Ailnoth had ended in the pool with a broken head. And who could avoid making the simple connection now? Who that had not spent so many days in Ninian's blithe company as had Cadfael, and got to know him so well?

'And after you had left him,' said Hugh, eyeing Giffard steadily, 'he knew the time and place appointed for you to meet with Bachiler, and the invitation you had rejected you think he went to accept? But without an acceptance from you, would Bachiler keep the appointment?'

'I made no answer. I had not rejected it outright. He was asking for help, for news, for a horse. He would come! He could not afford not to come.'

And he would meet with a very formidable and very angry enemy, bent on betraying him to the law, a man who verily held himself to be the instrument of the wrath of God. Yes, death could well come of such a meeting.

'Will,' said Hugh, turning abruptly to his sergeant, 'get back to the castle and bring down more men. We'll get the lord abbot's permission to search the gardens here, and the stables and the barns, grange court, storehouses, all. Begin with the mill, and have a watch on the bridge and the highway. If this youngster was in the hut here not half an hour ago, as Cadfael says, he cannot be far. And whether he has killed or no is still open, but the first need is to lay hands on him and have him safe in hold.'

'You will not forget,' said Cadfael, alone with Hugh in the workshop later, 'that there are others, many others, who had as good reason as Ninian, and better, to wish Ailnoth dead?'

'I don't forget it. Far too many others,' agreed Hugh ruefully. 'And all you tell me of this boy – not that I'm dull enough, mind, to suppose you've told me all you could! – shows him as one who might very well hit out boldly in his own defence, but scarcely from behind. Yet he might, in the

106

heat of conflict. Who knows what any of us might do, in extremes? And by what I hear of the priest, he would lash out with all his might and whatever weapon came to hand. It's the lad's vanishing now that suggests the worst.'

'He had good reason to vanish,' pointed out Cadfael, 'if he heard that Giffard was on his way to the castle to betray him. You'd have had to clap him into prison, guilty or innocent of the priest's death. Your hand's forced. Of course he'd run.'

'*If* someone warned him,' agreed Hugh with a wry smile. 'You, for instance?'

'No, not I,' said Cadfael virtuously. 'I knew nothing about Giffard's errand, or I might have dropped a word in the boy's ear. But no, certainly not I. I do know that Benet – Ninian we must call him now, I suppose! – was in the church some time before midnight on Christmas Eve. If he went to the mill at all, he went early for the meeting, and left early, also.'

'So you told me, and I believe it. But so, by your own account, did Ailnoth go early to the meeting place, perhaps to hide himself and spring out on Bachiler by surprise. There was still time for them to clash and one to die.'

'The boy had not the marks of any agitation or dismay upon him in the church. A little excitement, perhaps, but pleasurable, I would say. And how much have you managed to worm out of the parish folk about this business? There are a number who had justifiable grudges against Ailnoth, what have they to say for themselves?'

'In general, as you'd expect, as little as possible. One or two make no secret of their gratitude that the man's gone, none at all. Eadwin, the one whose boundary stone he moved, he's neither forgotten nor forgiven, even if the stone was replaced afterwards. His wife and children swear he never left the house that night – but so do they all, and so, of course, they would. Jordan Achard, the baker, now there's a man who might kill in a rage. He has a real grievance. His bread is his pride, and there was never any amends made for that insult. It hurt far more than if the priest had denounced him for a notorious lecher, which would at least have had the merit of being true. There are some give him the credit for being the father of that poor girl's baby, the lass who drowned herself, but from all I hear it could as well have been half the other men in the parish, for she couldn't say no to any of them. Our Jordan says he was home and sober every moment of Christmas Eve, and his wife bears him out, but she's a poor, subdued creature who wouldn't dare cross him. But from all accounts it's few nights he does spend in his own bed, and to judge by his wife's sidelong looks and wary answers he may well have been sleeping abroad that night. But we shall never get her to say so. She's both afraid of him and loyal to him.'

'The rest of his women may be less so,' said Cadfael. 'But I hardly see Jordan as a man of violence.'

'Perhaps not. But I do see Father Ailnoth as a man of violence, whether bodily or spiritual. And consider, Cadfael, how he might behave if he happened on one of his flock sneaking into the wrong bed. If not a violent man, Jordan is a big and strong one, and by no means meek enough to suffer assault tamely. He might end the fight another man began, without ever meaning to. But Jordan is one among many, and not the most likely.'

'Your men have been diligent,' said Cadfael with a sigh.

'They have. Alan was on his mettle, and determined to deserve his place. There's a decent poor soul called Centwin, who lives along the Foregate towards the horse-fair ground. You'll have heard his story. It was new to me until I heard it from Alan. The babe that died unchristened because Ailnoth could not interrupt his prayers. That sticks in the craw of every man in the parish, worse than all.'

'You cannot have found out anything black against Centwin?' protested Cadfael. 'As quiet a creature as breathes, never a trouble to any.'

'Never with occasion until now. But this goes deep. And Centwin, quiet as he may be, is also deep. He keeps his own counsel, and broods over his own grievances. I've spoken with him. We questioned the watch on the town gate,

Christmas Eve,' said Hugh. 'They saw you go out, and you best know the time that was, and where you met the priest. They also saw Centwin go out not many minutes after you, on his way home, he said, from visiting a friend in the town to whom he owed a small debt. True enough, for the tanner he paid has confirmed it. He wanted, he said, to have all his affairs clear and all dues paid before he went to Matins, as indeed he did go, and left before Lauds for home. But you see how the time fits. One coming a few minutes behind you may also have met with Ailnoth, may have seen him turn from the Foregate along the path to the mill. There in darkness and loneliness, think, might not even a mild, submissive man with that wound burning in his belly have seen suddenly an opportunity to pay off yet another and a more bitter debt? And there was the time between then and Matins for two men to clash in the darkness, and one to die.'

'No,' said Cadfael, 'I do not believe it!'

'Because it would be one cruelty piled upon another? But such things happen. No, take heart, Cadfael, neither do I quite believe it, but it is *possible*. There are too many by far who are not vouched for, or whose guarantors cannot be trusted, too many who hated him. And there is still Ninian Bachiler. Whatever the truth of him, you do understand that I must do my best to find him?'

He looked down at his friend with a dark, private smile that was more eloquent than the words. It was not the first time they had agreed, with considerate courtesy and no need of many words, to pursue each what he held to be his own duty, and bear no malice if the two crossed like swords.

'Oh, yes!' said Cadfael. 'Yes, that I fully understand.'

Chapter Eight

Cadfael had returned to the church after Prime to replenish the perfumed oil in the lamp on Saint Winifred's altar. The inquisitive skills which might have been frowned upon if they had been employed to make scents for women's vanity became permissible and even praiseworthy when used as an act of worship, and he took pleasure in trying out all manner of fragrant herbs and flowers in many different combinations, plying the sweets of rose and lily, violet and clover against the searching aromatic riches of rue and sage and wormwood. It pleased him to think that the lady must take delight in being so served, for virgin saint though she might be, she was a woman, and in her youth had been a beautiful and desirable one.

Cynric the verger came in from the north porch with the twig broom in his hand, from brushing away the night's sprinkling of fine snow from porch and steps, and went to open the great service-book on the reading desk, and trim the candles on the parish altar ready for the communal Mass, and set two new ones on the prickets of the wall brackets on either side. Cadfael gave him good day as he came back into the nave, and got the usual tranquil but brief acknowledgement.

'Freezing as hard as ever,' said Cadfael. 'There'll be no breaking the ground for Ailnoth today.' For it would be Cynric who had to dig the grave, in the green enclosure east of the church, where priests and abbots and brothers were laid to rest.

Cynric sniffed the air and considered, his deep eyes veiled.

'A change by tomorrow, maybe. I smell a thaw coming.'

It could be true. He lived on close, if neutral, terms with the elements, tolerating them as they seemed to refrain from harming him, for it must be deathly cold in that small, stony room over the porch.

'The ground's chosen for him?' asked Cadfael, catching the taciturn habit.

'Close under the wall.'

'Not next to Father Adam, then? I thought Prior Robert would have wanted to put him there.'

'He did,' said Cynric shortly. 'I said the earth there was not yet settled, and must have time to bed down.'

'A pity the hard frost came now. A dead man still lying among us unburied makes the young ones uneasy.'

'Ay,' said Cynric. 'The sooner he's in the ground the better for all. Now that he's gone.' He straightened the second thick candle on its spike, stepped back to make sure it stood erect and would not gutter, and brushed the clinging feel of tallow from his hands, for the first time turning his eyes in their hollow caverns upon Cadfael, and lighting up his lantern countenance with the smile of singular if rueful sweetness that brought the children to him with such serene confidence. 'Do you go into the Foregate this morning? I heard there's a few folk having trouble with the cold.'

'No wonder they should!' said Cadfael. 'I'm away to have a look at one or two of the children, but there's no great harm yet. Why, do you know of someone who needs me? I have leave, I can as well make one more visit. Who is sick?'

'It's the little wooden hovel on the left, along the back lane from the horse-fair, the widow Nest. She's caring for her grandchild, the poor worm, Eluned's baby, and she's fretted for it.' Cynric, perforce, was unusually loquacious in explaining. 'Won't take its milk, and cries with the wind in its belly.'

'It was born a healthy child?' asked Cadfael. For it could not be many weeks old, and motherless, deprived of its best food. He had not forgotten the shock and anger that had swept through the Foregate, when they lost their favourite whore. If indeed Eluned had ever been a whore. She never asked payment. If men gave her things, it was of their own will. She, it seemed, had done nothing but give, however unwisely.

'A bonny girl, big and lusty, so Nest said.'

'Then she'll have it in her, infant though she may be, to fight her way into life,' said Cadfael comfortably. 'I must go get the right cordial for an infant's inside. I'll make it fresh. Who sings Mass for you today?'

'Brother Anselm.'

'Well for you!' said Brother Cadfael, making for the south porch and his quickest way to the garden and his workshop. 'It might as easily have been Brother Jerome.'

The house was low and narrow, but sturdy, and the dark passage in which it stood braced against a taller dwelling looked crisp and clean in the hard frost, though in moist, mild weather it might have been an odorous hole. Cadfael rapped at the door, and for immediate reassurance called out loudly: 'Brother Cadfael from the abbey, mistress. Cynric said you need me for the child.'

Whether it was his own name or Cynric's that made him welcome there was no knowing, but instantly there was a stir of movement within, a baby howled fretfully, probably at being laid down in haste, and then the door was opened wide, and from half-darkness a woman beckoned him within, and made haste to close the door after him against the cold.

This one small room was all the house, and its only inlet for light or outlet for smoke was a vent in the roof. In clement weather the door would always be open from dawn to dusk, but frost had closed it, and the dwelling was lit only by a small oil lamp and the dim but steady glow of a fire penned in an iron cage on a flat stone under the vent. But blessedly someone had supplied charcoal for the widow's needs, and there was a mild fume in the nostrils here but little smoke. Furnishings were few, a low bench-bed in a corner, a few pots on the firestone, a rough, small table. Cadfael took a little time to accustom his eyes to the dim light, and the shapes of things emerged gradually. The woman stood by him, waiting, and like all else here, grew steadily out of the gloom, a perceptible human being. The cradle, the central concern of this house, was placed in the most sheltered corner, where the warmth of the fire could come, but not the draught from door or vent. And the child within was wailing indignantly within its wrappings, half-asleep but unable by reason of discomfort to fall deeper into peace.

'I brought an end of candle with me,' said Cadfael, taking in everything about him without haste. 'I thought we might need more light. With your leave!' He took it out from his scrip, tilted the wick into the small flame of the lamp in its clay saucer, and stood the stump upon the corner of the table, where it shed light closely upon the cradle. It was a broad-based end discarded from one of the prickets in the wall brackets of the church, he found them useful for carrying on his errands because they would stand solidly on any flat surface, and run no risk of being overturned. Among flimsy wooden cottages there was need of such care. This dwelling, poor as it was, had been more solidly built than many.

'They keep you in charcoal?' asked Cadfael, turning to the woman, who stood quite still, gazing at him with fixed and illusionless eyes.

'My man who's dead was a forester in Eyton. The abbey's man there remembers me. He brings me wood, as well, the dead twigs and small chippings for kindling.'

'That's well,' said Cadfael. 'So young a babe needs to be kept warm. Now you tell me, what's her trouble?'

She was telling him herself, in small, fretful wails from her cradle, but she was well wrapped and clean, and had a healthy, well-nourished voice with which to complain.

'Three days now she's sickened on her milk, and cries with the wind inside. But I've kept her warm, and she's taken no chill. If my poor girl had lived this chit would have been at her breast, not sipping from a spoon or my fingers, but she's gone, and left this one to me, all I have now, and I'll do anything to keep her safe.'

'She's been feeding well enough, by the look of her,' said Cadfael, stooping over the whimpering child. 'How old is she now? Six weeks is it, or seven? She's big and bonny for that age.'

The small, contorted face, all wailing mouth and tight-shut eyes screwed up with annoyance, was round and clear-skinned, though red now with exertion and anger. She had abundant, fine hair of a bright autumn brown, and inclined to curl.

'Feed well, yes, indeed she did, until this upset. A greedy-gut, even. I was proud of her.'

And kept plying her too long, thought Cadfael, and she without the sense yet to know when she had enough. No great mystery here.

'That's a part of her trouble, you'll find. Give her only a little at a time, and often, and put in the milk a few drops of the cordial I'll leave with you. Three or four drops will be enough. Get me a small spoon, and she shall have a proper dose of it now to soothe her.'

The widow brought him a little horn spoon, and he unstoppered the glass bottle he had brought, moistened the tip of a finger at its lip, and touched it to the lower lip of the baby's angry mouth. In an instant the howling broke off short, and the contorted countenance resumed a human shape, and even a human expression of wonder and surprise. The mouth closed, small moist lips folding on an unexpected sweetness; and miraculously this became a mouth too shapely and delicate for a baby of seven weeks, with a distant promise of beauty. The angry red faded slowly to leave the round cheeks flushed with rose, and Eluned's daughter opened great eyes of a blue almost as dark as the night sky, and smiled an aware, responsive smile, too old for her few weeks of life. True, she wrinkled her face and uttered a warning wail the next moment, but the far-off vision of loveliness remained.

'The creature!' said her grandmother, ruefully fond. 'She likes it!'

Cadfael half-filled the little spoon, touched it gently to the baby's lower lip, and instantly her mouth opened, willing to suck in the offering. It went down fairly tidily, leaving only a gloss upon the relaxed lips. She gazed upward in silence for a moment, from those eyes that devoured half her face under the rounded brow and fluff of auburn hair. Then she turned her cheek a little into the flat pillow under her, belched resoundingly, and lay quiescent with lids half-closed, her infinitesimal fingers curled into small, easy fists under her chin.

'Nothing amiss with her that need cause you any worry,' said Cadfael, re-stoppering the bottle. 'If she wakes and cries in the night, and is again in pain, you can give her a little of this in the spoon, as I did. But I think she'll sleep. Give her somewhat less food at a time than you've been giving, and put three or four drops of this in the milk, and we'll see how she fares in a few days more.'

'What is in it?' asked the widow, looking curiously at the bottle in her hand.

'There's dill, fennel, mint, just a morsel of poppy-juice . . . and honey to make it agreeable to the taste. Put it somewhere safe and use it as I've said. If she's again troubled this way, give her the dose you saw me give. If she does well enough without it, then spare it but for the drop or two in her food. Medicines are of more effect if used only when there's need.'

He blew out the end of candle he had brought, leaving it to cool and congeal, for it had still an hour or so of burning left in it, and could serve again in the same office. On the instant he was sorry he had diminished the light in the room so soon, for only now had he leisure to look at the woman. This was the widowed mother of the girl who had been shut out of the church as an irredeemable sinner, whose very penitence and confession were not to be trusted, and therefore could justifiably be rejected. Out of this small, dark dwelling that disordered beauty had blossomed, borne fruit, and died.

The mother must herself have been comely, some years ago, she had still fine features, though worn and lined now in shapes of discouragement, and her greying hair, drawn back austerely from her face, was still abundant, and bore the shadowy richness of its former red-brown colouring. There was no saying whether the dark, hollow eyes that studied her grandchild with such a bitter burden of love were dark blue, but they well might have been. She was probably barely forty. Cadfael had seen her about the Foregate now and then, but never before paid close attention to her.

'A fine babe you have there,' said Cadfael. 'She may well grow into a beautiful child.'

'Better she should be plain as any drab,' said the widow with abrupt passion, 'than take after her mother's beauty, and go the same way. You do know whose child she is? Everyone knows it!'

'No fault of this little one she left behind,' said Cadfael. 'I hope the world will treat her better than it treated her mother.'

'It was not the world that cast her off,' said Nest, 'but the church. She could have lived under the world's malice, but not when the priest shut her out of the church.'

'Did her worship truly mean so much to her,' asked Cadfael gravely, 'that she could not live excommunicate?'

'Truly it did. You never knew her! As wild and rash as she was beautiful, but such a bright, kind, warm creature to have about the house, and for all her wildness she was easily hurt. She who never could bear to wound any other creature was open to wounds herself. But for the thing she could not help, no one could have been a better and sweeter daughter to me. You can't know how it was! She could not refuse to anyone whatever he asked of her, if it was in her power to give it. And the men found it out, and having no shame – for sin was something she spoke of without understanding – she could

116

not say no to men, either. She would go with a man because he was melancholy, or because he begged her, or because he had been blamed or beaten unjustly and was aggrieved at the world. And then it would come over her that this might indeed be sin, as Father Adam had told her, though she could not see why. And then she went flying to confession, in tears, and promised amendment, and meant it, too. Father Adam was gentle with her, seeing she was not like other young women. He always spoke her kindly and fair, and gave her light penance, and never refused her absolution. Always she promised to amend, but then she forgot for some boy's light tongue or dark eyes, and sinned again, and again confessed and was shriven. She couldn't keep from men, but neither could she live without the blessing and comfort of the church. When the door was shut in her face she went solitary away, and solitary she died. And for all she was a torment to me, living, she was a joy, too, and now I have only torment, and no joy – but for this fearful joy here in the cradle. Look, she's asleep!'

'Do you know,' asked Cadfael, brooding, 'who fathered the child?'

Nest shook her head, and a faint, dry smile plucked at her lips. 'No. As soon as she understood it might bring blame on him, whoever he was, she kept him a secret even from me. If, indeed, she knew herself which one of them had quickened her! Yet I think she did know. She was neither mad nor dull of understanding. She was brighter than most, but for the part of caution that was left out of her. She might have confronted the man to his face, but she would never betray him to the black priest. Oh, he asked her! He threatened her, he raged at her, but she said that for her sins she would answer and do penance, but another man's sins were his own, and so must his confession be.'

A good answer! Cadfael acknowledged it with a nod and a sigh.

The candle was cold and set. He restored it to his scrip, and turned to take his leave. 'Well, if she's fretful again and you need me, let me know of it by Cynric, or leave word at the gatehouse, and I'll come. But I think you'll find the cordial will serve your turn.' He looked back for a second with his hand on the latch of the door. 'What have you named her? Eluned, for her mother?'

'No,' said the widow. 'It was Eluned chose her name. Praise God, it was Father Adam who christened her, before he fell ill and died. She's called Winifred.'

Cadfael walked back along the Foregate with that last echo still ringing in his mind. The daughter of the outcast and excommunicate, it seemed, was named for the town's own saint, witness enough to the truth of Eluned's undisciplined devotion. And doubtless Saint Winifred would know where to find and watch over both the living child and the dead mother, whom the parish of Saint Chad, more prodigally merciful than Father Ailnoth, had buried decently, observing a benevolent Christian doubt concerning the circumstances of her unwitnessed death. A strong strain, these Welsh women married into Shropshire families. He knew nothing of the English forester who had been husband to the widow Nest, but surely it must be she who had handed on to her self-doomed child the fierce beauty that had been her downfall, and the same face, in prophetic vision, waited for the infant Winifred in her cradle. Perhaps the choice of her venerated name had been a brave gesture to protect a creature otherwise orphaned and unprotected, a waif in an alien world where too prodigal a union of beauty and generosity brought only grief.

Now there, in the cottage he had left behind, was one being who had the best of all reasons to hate Ailnoth, and might have killed him if a thought could have done it, but was hardly likely to follow him through the winter night and strike him down from behind, much less roll him, stunned, into the pool. She had too powerful a lodestone to keep her watchful and protective at home. But the vengeful fire in her might drive a man to do it for her sake, if she had so close and resolute a friend. Among all those men who had taken comfort from the world's spite in Eluned's arms, might there not be more than one ready and willing? And in particular, if he knew what seed he had sown, the father of the infant Winifred.

At this rate, thought Cadfael, mildly irritated with his own preoccupation, I shall be looking sidewise at every comely man I see, to try if I can find in his face any resemblance to a murderer. I'd best concern myself with my own duties, and leave official retribution to Hugh – not that he'll be grateful for it!

He was approaching the gatehouse, and had just come to the entrance to the twisting alley that led to the priest's house. He halted there, suddenly aware that the heavy covering cloud had lifted, and a faint gleam of sun showed through. Not brilliantly and icily out of a pale, cold sky, but timidly and grudgingly through untidy, wallowing shreds of cloud. The glitter coruscating from icicles and swags of frozen snow along the eaves had acquired a softer, moist brightness. There was even a drip here and there from a gable end where the timorous sun fell. Cynric might be right in his prediction, and a thaw on the way by nightfall. Then they could at least put Ailnoth out of the chapel and under the ground, though his baleful shadow would still be with them.

There was no haste to return to the abbey and his workshop, half an hour more would not do any harm. Cadfael turned into the alley and walked along to the priest's house. He was none too sure of his own motives in paying this visit. Certainly it was his legitimate business to make sure that Mistress Hammet's injuries had healed properly, and she had taken no lingering harm from the blow to her head, but pure curiosity had a part in what prompted him, too. Here was another woman whose attitude to Father Ailnoth might be exceedingly ambivalent, torn between gratitude for a patronage which had given her status and security, and desperation at his raging resentment of the deception practised on him, if she knew how he had found it out, and his all too probable intent to see her nurseling unmasked and thrown into prison. Cadfael's judgement of Diota was that she went in considerable awe and fear of her master, but also that she would dare much for the boy she had nursed. But any suspicion of her was quickly tempered by his recollection of her state on Christmas morning. Almost certainly, whatever her fears after a night of waiting in vain, she had not known that Ailnoth was dead until the searchers returned with his body. As often as Cadfael told himself he could be deceived in believing that, his own memory rejected the doubt.

Just beyond the priest's house the narrow alley opened out into a small grassy space, now a circle of trampled rime, but with the green of grass peeping through by small, indomitable tufts here and there. To this confined playground the house presented its fine, unbroken wall, the one that attracted the players of ball games and the like, to their peril. There were half a dozen urchins of the Foregate playing there now, rolling snowballs and hurling them from an ambitiously remote mark at a target set up on an abandoned fence-post at the corner of the green. A round black cap, with a fluttering end of torn braid quivering in the light wind. A skull cap, such as a priest would wear, or a monk, to cover his tonsure from cold when the cowl was inconvenient.

One small possession of Ailnoth's which had not been recovered with him, nor missed. Cadfael stood and gazed, remembering sharply the clear image of the priest's set and formidable face as he passed the gatehouse torches, unshadowed by any cowl, and capped, yes, certainly capped in black, this meagre circle that cast no shadows, but left his apocalyptic rage plain to view.

One of the marksmen, luckier or more adroit, had knocked the target flying into the grass. The victor, without great interest now, having prevailed, went to pick it up, and stood dangling it in one hand, while the rest of the band, capricious as children can be, burst into a spirited argument as to what they should do next, and like a wisp of snipe rising, suddenly took off across the grass towards the open field beyond.

The marksman made to follow them, but with no haste, knowing they would settle as abruptly as they had taken flight, and he could be up with them whenever he willed. Cadfael went a few paces to intercept his passage, and the boy halted readily enough, knowing him. A bright boy, ten years old, the reeve's sister's son. He had a charming, inscrutable smile.

'What's that you have there, Eddi?' asked Cadfael, nodding at the dangling cap. 'May I see it?'

It was handed over willingly, indifferently. No doubt they had played various games with it for several days now, and were weary of it. Some other brief foundling toy would take its place, and it would never be missed. Cadfael turned it in his hands, and marked how the braid that bound its rim was ripped clear on one side, and dangled the loose end. When he drew it into place there was still a strand missing, perhaps the length of his little finger, and the stitching of two of the segments that made up the circle had been frayed apart with the lost shred. Good black cloth, carefully made, the braid hand-plaited wool.

'Where did you find this, Eddi?'

'In the mill-pond,' said the boy readily. 'Someone threw it away because it was torn. We went down early in the morning to see if the pond was frozen, but it wasn't. But we found this.'

'Which morning was that?' asked Cadfael.

'Christmas Day. It was only just getting light.' The boy was grave, demure of countenance, impenetrable as clever children can be.

'Where in the mill-pond? On the mill side?'

'No, we went along the other path, where it's shallow. That's where it freezes first. The tail-race keeps it open the other side.'

So it did, the movement enough to preserve an open channel until all froze over, and the same stream of moving water would carry a light thing, like this cap, over to lodge in the shallows.

'This was caught among the reeds there?'

The boy said yes, serenely.

'You know whose this is, do you, Eddi?'

'No, sir,' said Eddi, and smiled a brief, guileless smile. He was, Cadfael recalled, one of those unfortunate children who had been learning their letters with Father Adam, and had fallen into less tolerant hands after his death. And wronged and injured children are not themselves merciful to their tyrants.

'No matter, son. Are you done with it? Will you leave it with me? I'll bring you a few apples to your father's, a fair exchange. And you may forget it.'

'Yes, sir,' said the boy, and turned and skipped away without another glance, rid of his prize and his burden.

Cadfael stood looking down at the small, drab thing in his hands, damp now and darkening from the comparative warmth of being handled, but fringed with rime and still stiff. How unlike Father Ailnoth to be seen wearing a cap with a tattered braid and a seam beginning to lose its stitches! If, indeed, it had been in this condition when he put it on? It had been tossed around at random since Christmas Day, and might have come by its dilapidations at any time since it was plucked out of the frosty reeds, where the drift of the tail-race had carried it, while the heavier body from which it had been flung was gradually edged aside under the leaning bank.

And was there not something else that had been forgotten, as this cap had been forgotten? Something else they should have looked for, and had never thought of? Something nagging at the back of Cadfael's mind but refusing to show itself?

He thrust the cap into his scrip, and turned back to rap at the door of the priest's house. It was opened to him by Diota, prim and composed in her customary black. She stepped back readily, unsmiling but hospitable, and beckoned him at once into a small, warm room dimly lit by a brownish light from two small windows, into the shutters of which thin sheets of horn had been set. A bright wood fire burned on the clay hearth in the centre of the room, and on the cushioned bench beside it a young woman was sitting, alert and silent, and to one entering from broad daylight not immediately recognisable.

'I came only to ask how you are,' said Cadfael as the door was closed behind him, 'and to see if you need anything more for your grazes.'

Diota came round to face him and let herself be seen, the palest of smiles visiting a face habitually grave and anxious. 'That was kind of you, Brother Cadfael. I am well, I thank you, quite well. You see the wound is healed.'

She turned her injured temple docilely to the best of the light at the urging of his hand, and let him study what had faded now to a yellow bruise and a small dry scar.

'Yes, that's well, there'll be no mark left to show for it. But I should go on using the ointment for a few days yet, in this frost the skin dries and abrades easily. And you've had no headaches?'

'No, none.'

'Good! Then I'll be off back to my work, and not take up your time, for I see you have a visitor.'

'Oh, no,' said the visitor, rising briskly from the bench, 'I was about to take my leave.' She stepped forward, raising to the light a rounded young face, broad at the brow and tapering gently to a resolute chin. Challenging harebell-blue eyes, set very wide apart, confronted Cadfael with a direct and searching stare. 'If you must really go so soon,' said Sanan Bernières, with the serene confidence of a masterful child, 'I'll walk with you. I've been waiting to find a right time to talk to you.'

There was no gainsaying such a girl. Diota did not venture to try and detain her, and Brother Cadfael, even if he had wished, would have hesitated before denying her. Law itself, he thought with amused admiration, might come off the loser if it collided with the will of Sanan Bernières. In view of

123

all that had happened, that was a distinct if as yet distant possibility, but she would not let the prospect deter her.

'That will be great pleasure for me,' said Cadfael. 'The walk is very short – but perhaps you'll be needing some more herbs for your kitchen? I have ample supplies, you may come in and take what you wish.'

She did give him a very sharp glance for that, and as suddenly dimpled, and to hide laughter turned to embrace Diota, kissing her thin cheek like a daughter. Then she drew her cloak about her and led the way out into the alley, and together they walked the greater part of the way out into the Foregate in silence.

'Do you know,' she said then, 'why I went to see Mistress Hammet?'

'Out of womanly sympathy, surely,' said Cadfael, 'with her loss. Loss and loneliness – still a virtual stranger here . . .'

'Oh, come!' said Sanan bluntly. 'She worked for the priest, I suppose it was a secure life for a widow woman, but loss . . .? Lonely she may well be.'

'I was not speaking of Father Ailnoth,' said Cadfael.

She gave him another straight glance of her startling blue eyes, and heaved a thoughtful sigh. 'Yes, you've worked with him, you know him. He told you, didn't he, that she was his nurse, no blood kin? She never had children in her own marriage, he's as dear as a son to her. I . . . have talked with him, too – by chance. You know he sent a message to my step-father. Everyone knows that now. I was curious to see this young man, that's all.'

They had reached the abbey gatehouse. She stood hesitant, frowning at the ground.

'Now everyone is saying that he – this Ninian Bachiler – killed Father Ailnoth, because the priest was going to betray him to the sheriff. I knew she must have heard it. I knew she would be alone, afraid for him, now he's fled, and hunted for his life – for it *is* his life, now!'

'So you came to bear her company,' said Cadfael, 'and reassure her. Come through into the garden, and if you have all the pot-herbs you want, I daresay we can find another good reason. You won't be any the worse for having something by you to cure the cough that may be coming along in a week or two.'

She looked up with a flashing smile. 'The same remedy you gave me when I was ten? I've changed so much you can hardly have known me again. Such excellent health I have, I need you only once every seven or eight years.'

'If you need me now,' said Cadfael simply, leading the way across the great court towards the gardens, 'that's enough.'

She followed demurely, lowering her eyes modestly in this male seclusion, and in the safe solitude of the workshop she allowed herself to be installed comfortably with her small feet towards the brazier before she drew breath again and went on talking, now more freely, having left all other ears outside the door.

'I came to see Mistress Hammet because I was afraid that, now that he is so threatened, she might do something foolish. She is devoted to Ninian, in desperation she might do anything – *anything!* – to ensure that he goes free. She might even come forward with some mad story about being to blame herself. She would, I am sure, for him! If she thought it would clear him of all guilt, she would confess to murder.'

'So you came,' said Cadfael, moving about his private world quietly to leave her the illusion that she was not closely observed, 'to urge her to hold her peace and wait calmly, for he's still at liberty and in no immediate danger. Is that it?'

'Yes. And if you go to see her again, or she comes to you, please urge the same upon her. Don't let her do anything to harm herself.'

'Did he send you, to see her and tell her this?' asked Cadfael directly.

She was not yet quite ready to be drawn into the open, though fleetingly she smiled. 'It's simply that I know, I understand, how anxious he must be now about her. He would be glad if he knew I had talked to her.'

As he will know, before many hours are out, thought Cadfael. Now I wonder where she has hidden him? There could well be old retainers of her own father here in Shrewsbury, or close by, men who would do a great deal for Bernières's daughter.

'I know,' said Sanan with slow solemnity, following Cadfael's movements with intent eyes, 'that you discovered Ninian before ever my step-father betrayed him. I know he told you freely who he is and what he's about, and you said you had nothing against any honest man of either party, and would do nothing to harm him. And you've kept his secret until now, when it's no longer a secret. He trusts you, and I am resolved to trust you.'

'No,' said Cadfael hastily, 'tell me nothing! If I don't know where the boy is now, no one can get it out of me, and I can declare my ignorance with a good conscience. I like a gallant lad, even if he is too rash for his own good. He tells me his whole aim now is to reach the Empress, at whatever cost, and offer her his services. He has a right to dispose of his own efforts as he pleases, and I wish him a safe arrival and long life. Such a madcap deserves to have luck on his side.'

'I know,' she said, flushing and smiling, 'he is not very discreet. . . .'

'Discreet? I doubt if he knows the meaning of the word! To write and send such a letter, open as the day, signed with his own name and telling where and under what pretence he's to be found! No, never tell me where he is now, but wherever you've hidden him, keep a weather eye on him, for there's no knowing what breathless foolishness he'll be up to next.' He had been busy filling a small flask, to provide her with a respectable reason for emerging from his herbarium. He sealed it with a wooden stopper and tied it down at the neck under a wisp of thin parchment before wrapping it in a piece of linen and putting it into her hands. 'There, madam, is your permit to be here. And my advice is, get him away as soon as you can.'

'But he won't go,' she said, sighing, but with pride rather than exasperation, 'not while this matter is unresolved. He won't budge until he knows Diota is safe. And there are preparations to make – means to provide. . . .' She shook herself bracingly, tossed her brown head, and made briskly for the door.

'His first need,' said Cadfael thoughtfully after her, 'will be a good horse.'

She turned about abruptly in the doorway, and gave him a blazing smile, throwing aside all reservations.

'Two horses!' she said in a soft, triumphant whisper. 'I am of the Empress's party, too. I am going with him!'

Chapter Nine

Cadfael was uneasy in his mind all that day, plagued on the one hand by misgivings about Sanan's revelation, and on the other by the elusive gnat that sang in the back of his consciousness, telling him persistently that he had failed to notice the loss of one item that should have been sought with Ailnoth, and might very well have missed another. There was certainly something he should have thought of, something that might shed light, if only he could discover what it was, and go, belatedly, to look for it.

In the meantime, he pursued the round of his duties through Vespers and supper in the refectory, and tried in vain to concentrate upon the psalms for this thirtieth day of December, the sixth day in the octave of Christmas.

Cynric had been right about the thaw. It came furtively and grudgingly, but it was certainly on its way by mid afternoon. The trees were shedding their tinkling filigree of frozen rime and standing starkly black against a low sky. Drips perforated the whiteness under the eaves with small dark pockmarks, and the black of the road and the green of grass were beginning to show through the covering of snow. By morning it might even be possible to break the ground, in that chosen spot sheltered under the precinct wall, and dig Father Ailnoth's grave.

Cadfael had examined the skull-cap closely, and could make no great sense of it. Yet it fretted him simply because he had failed to think of it when the body was found. As for the damage to it, that suggested a connection with the blow to the head, and yet at the same time contradicted that connection, since in that event the cap would surely have fallen on land, when the blow was struck. True, the assailant might very well have thrown it into the water after the priest, but in the dark would he have noticed or thought of it, and if he had, would he necessarily have been able to find it? A small black thing in tufted grass not yet white with rime – not easy to see, and unlikely to be remembered as too dangerous to leave, when murder had been committed. Who was going to grope around in the dark in rough grass, when he had just killed a man? His one thought would be to get well away from the scene as quickly as possible.

Well, if Cadfael had missed this one thing, he might have missed – his demon was nagging at him that he *had* missed! – another as important. And if he had, it was still there by the mill, either along the bank or in the water, or even within the mill itself. No use looking for it elsewhere.

There was half an hour left before Compline, and most of the brothers, very sensibly, were in the warming room, getting the chill out of their bones. It was folly to think of going near the mill at this hour, in the dark, but for all that Cadfael could not keep away, his mind so dwelt upon the place, as though the very ambience of the pool, the mill and the solitary night might reproduce the events of Christmas Eve, and prod his memory into recapturing the lost factor. He crossed the great court to the retired corner by the infirmary, where the wicket in the precinct wall led through directly to the mill.

Outside, with no moon and only ragged glimpses of stars, he stood until his eyes grew accustomed to the night, and the shapes of things grew out of obscurity. The rough grass of the field, the dark bulk of the mill to his right, with the little wooden bridge at the corner of the building immediately before him, crossing the head-race to the overhanging bank of the pool. He crossed, his feet making a small, clear, hollow sound on the planks, and walked across the narrow strip of grass to the bank. The expanse of the water opened beneath him, pale, leaden-still, dappled with patches of open water, rimmed round with half-thawed ice.

Nothing moved here but himself, there was nothing to be heard, not even a breath of wind stirring in the lissome naked shoots of the pollarded willows at his left hand along the bank. A few yards along there, just past the nearest stump, cut down to hip-height and bristling with wands like hair on the giant head of a terrified man, they had drawn Ailnoth's body laboriously along under the eroded bank, and brought him to shore where the meadow sloped down more gently to the outflow of the tail-race.

In his recollection of the morning every detail stood sharply defined, but shed no light at all on what had happened in the night. He turned from the high bank and walked back across the bridge, and for no good reason that he could see continued round the mill, and down the sloping bank to the big doors where the grain was carried in. Only an outer bar fastened the door, and that, he saw dimly by the faint reflection from bleached timber, was drawn back from its socket. There was a small door on the higher level, giving quick access to the wicket in the precinct wall. That could be fastened within. But why should this heavy bar be drawn back unless someone had made entry from without?

Cadfael set his hand to the closed but unbarred door, eased it open by a hand's breadth, and stiffened to listen with an ear to the chink. Nothing but silence from within. He opened it a little wider, slid quietly through, and eased the door back again behind him. The warm scents of flour and grain tickled his nostrils. He had a nose sharp as fox or hound, and trusted to it in the dark, and there was another scent here, very faint, utterly familiar. In his own workshop he was unaware of it from long and constant acquaintance, but in any other place it pricked his consciousness with a particular insistence, as of a stolen possession of his own, and a valued one, that had no business to stray. A man cannot be in and out of a workshop saturated with years of harvesting herbs, and not carry the scent of them about in his garments. Cadfael froze with his back against the closed door, and waited.

The faintest stir reached his ears, as of a foot carefully placed in dust and husk that could not choose but rustle, however cautiously trodden. Somewhere above him, on the upper floor. So the hatch was open, and someone was leaning there, carefully shifting his stance to drop through. Cadfael moved obligingly in that direction, to give him encouragement. Next moment a body dropped neatly behind him, and an arm clamped about his neck, bracing him back against his assailant, while its fellow embraced him about chest and arms, pinning him close. He stood slack within the double grip, and continued to breathe easily, and with wind to spare.

'Not badly done,' he said with mild approval. 'But you have no nose, son. What are four senses, without the fifth?'

'Have I not?' breathed Ninian's voice in his ear, shaken by a quaver of suppressed laughter. 'You came in at the door so like a waft of wind through your eaves, I was back there with that oil I had to abandon. I hope it took no harm.' Hard and vehement young arms hugged Cadfael close, let him loose gently, and turned him about at arm's length, as though to view him, where there was no light to see more than a shape, a shadow. 'I owed you a fright. You had the wits scared out of me when you eased the door ajar,' said Ninian reproachfully.

'I was none too easy in my own mind,' said Cadfael, 'when I found the bar out of its socket. Lad, you take far too many chances. For God's sake and Sanan's, what are you doing here?'

'I could as well ask you that,' said Ninian. 'And might get the same answer, too. I ventured here to see if there was anything more to be found, though after so many days, heaven knows why there should be. But how can any of us be easy until we know? *I* know I never laid hands on the man, but what comfort is that when everyone else lays it at my door? I should be loth to leave here until it's shown I'm no murderer, even if there were nothing more in it than that, but there is. There's Diota! Wanting the chance to get at me, how long before they begin to turn on her, if not for murder, then for treason in helping me to escape the hunt in the south, and cover my guilt here?'

'If you think Hugh Beringar has any ill intent against Mistress Hammet, or will suffer anyone else to make her a victim,' said Cadfael firmly, 'you may put that out of your mind at once. Well, now, since we're both here, and the time and place as good as any, we may as well sit down somewhere in the warmest corner we can find, and put together whatever we have to share. Two heads may make more of it than my one has been able to do. There should be plenty of sacks here somewhere – better than nothing. . . .'

Evidently Ninian had been here long enough to know his way about, for he took Cadfael by the arm, and drew him confidently into a corner where a pile of clean, coarse bags was folded and stacked against the timber wall. They settled themselves close there, flank by flank for warmth, and Ninian drew round them both a thick cloak which had certainly never been in Benet's possession.

'Now,' said Cadfael briskly, 'I should first tell you that this very morning I've spoken with Sanan, and I know what you and she are planning. Probably she's told you as much. I'm half in and half out of your confidence and hers, and if I'm to be of any help to you in putting an end to this vexatious business that holds you here, you had better let me in fully. I do *not* believe you guilty of the priest's death, and I have no reason in the world to stand in your way. But I do believe that you know more of what happened here that night than you have told. Tell the rest, and let me know where we really stand. You did come here to the mill, did you not?'

Ninian blew out a gusty, rueful breath that warmed Cadfael's leaning cheek for a moment. 'I did. I had to. I got no more answer from Giffard than that he'd received and understood the message I sent. I'd no means of knowing whether he meant to come or not. But I came very early, to view the place and find a corner to hide in until I saw what came of it. I stayed there in the doorway in the abbey wall, with the wicket ajar, so that I could watch for whoever came. I had to make haste round the corner of the infirmary, I can tell you, when the miller came bustling through on his way to church, but I had the place to myself after that, to keep watch on the path.'

'And it was Ailnoth who came?' said Cadfael.

'Storming along the path like a bolt from God. Dark as it was, there was no mistaking him, he had a gait all his own. There was no possible reason he should be there at such an hour, unless he'd got wind of what I was up to, and meant all manner of mischief. He was striding up and down and round the mill and along the bank, thumping the ground like a cat lashing its tail. And I'd perhaps got another man into the mud with me, and must make some shift to get him, at least, out of it, even if I was still stuck in the mire.'

'So what did you do?'

'It was still early. I couldn't leave Giffard to come to the meeting all unsuspecting, could I? I didn't know if he meant to come at all, but still he might, I couldn't take the risk. I hared away back through the court and out at the gatehouse, and went to earth among the bushes close by the end of the bridge. If he came at all, he had to come that way from the town. And I didn't even know what the man looked like, though I knew his name and his allegiance from others. But I thought there'd be very few men coming out from the town at that hour, and I could risk accosting any who looked of his age and quality.'

'Ralph Giffard had already come over the bridge,' said Cadfael, 'a good hour earlier, to visit the priest and send him hot-foot to confront you at the mill, but you could hardly know that. I fancy he was already back in his own house while you were watching for him in the bushes. Did you see any others pass by you there?'

'Only one, and he was too young, and too poor and simple in his person and gear to be Giffard. He went straight along the Foregate, and turned in at the church.'

Centwin, perhaps, thought Cadfael, coming from paying

his debt, to have his mind free and at peace, owing no man, as he went to celebrate the birth of Christ. Well for him if it proved that Ninian could speak for him, and show clearly that his own bitter debt had gone unreclaimed.

'And you?'

'I waited until I was sure he was not coming – it was past the time. So I made haste back to be in time for Matins.'

'Where you met with Sanan.' Cadfael's smile was invisible in the dark, but perceptible in his voice. 'She was not so foolish as to go to the mill, for like you, she could not be quite sure her step-father would not keep the tryst. But she knew where to find you, and she was determined to respond to the appeal Giffard had preferred to reject. Indeed, as I recall, she had already taken steps to get a good look at you, as you yourself told me. Maybe you'll do for a lady's page, after all. With a little polishing!'

Within the muffling folds of the cloak he heard Ninian laughing softly. 'I never believed, that first day, that anything would really come of it. And now see – everything I owe to her. She would not be put off. . . . You've seen her, you've talked to her, you know how splendid she is. . . . Cadfael, I must tell you – she's coming with me to Gloucester, she's promised herself to me in marriage.' His voice was low and solemn now, as though he had already come to the altar. It was the first time Cadfael had known him in awe of anything or anyone.

'She is a very valiant lady,' said Cadfael slowly, 'and knows her own mind very well, and I, for my part, wouldn't say a word against her choice. But, lad, is it right to let her do this for you? Is she not abandoning property, family, everything? Have you considered that?'

'I have, and urged her to consider it, too. How much do you know, Cadfael, of her situation? She has no land to abandon. Her father's manor was taken from him after the siege here, because he supported FitzAlan and the Empress. Her mother is dead. Her step-father – she has no complaint of him, he has always cared for her in duty bound, but not

134

gladly. He has a son by his first marriage to inherit from him, he will be only too pleased to have an estate undivided, and to escape providing her a dowry. But from her mother she has a good provision in jewels, undeniably her own. She says she loses nothing by coming with me, and gains what she most wants in the world. I do love her!' said Ninian with abrupt and moving gravity. 'I will make a fit place for her. I can! I will!'

Yes, thought Cadfael on reflection, on balance she may be getting none so bad a bargain. Giffard himself lost certain lands for his adherence to the Empress, no wonder he wants all he has left to go to his son. It may even be more for his son's sake than his own that he has so ruthlessly severed himself now from any lingering devotion to his former overlord, and even sought to buy his own security with this boy's freedom. Men do things far out of their nature when deformed by circumstances. And the girl knew a good lad when she saw one, she'll be his fair match.

'Well, I wish you a fortunate journey through Wales, with all my heart,' he said. 'You'll need horses for the journey, is that already arranged?'

'We have them, she procured them. They're stabled where I'm in hiding,' said Ninian, candid and thoughtless, 'out by—'

Cadfael clapped a hand hastily over the boy's mouth, fumbling in the dark but effectively silencing him out of sheer surprise. 'No, hush, tell me nothing! Better I know nothing of where you are, or where you got your horses. What I don't know I can't even be expected to tell.'

'But I can't go,' said Ninian firmly, 'while there's a shadow hanging over me. I won't be remembered, here or anywhere, as a fugitive murderer. Still less can I go while there's such a shadow hanging over Diota. I owe her more already than I know how to repay, I must see her secure and protected before I go.'

'The more credit to you, and we must try by any means we have for a resolution. As it seems we've both been doing

135

tonight, though with very sorry success. But now, had you not best be getting back to your hiding place? How if Sanan should send to you, and you not there?'

'And you?' retorted Ninian. 'How if Prior Robert should make a round of the dortoir, and you not there?'

They rose together, and unwound the cloak from about them, drawing in breath sharply at the invading cold.

'You haven't told me,' said Ninian, opening the heavy door on the comparative light outside, 'just what thought brought you here tonight – though I'm glad it did. I was not happy at leaving you without a word. But you can hardly have been hunting for me! What were you hoping to find?'

'I wish I knew. This morning I found a gaggle of goslings playing in the snow with a black skull-cap that surely belonged to Ailnoth, for the boys had found it here in the shallows of the pool, among the reeds. And I had seen him wearing it that evening, and clean forgotten so small a thing. And it's been nagging at me all day long since then that there was something else I had noted about him, and likewise never missed and never looked for afterwards. I don't know that I came here with any great expectation of finding anything. Perhaps I simply hoped that being here might bring the thing back to mind. Did ever you get up to do something, and then clean forget what it was?' wondered Cadfael. 'And have to go back to where you first thought of it, to bring it back to mind? No, surely not, you're too young, for you to think of doing a thing is to do it. But ask the elders like me, they'll all admit to it.'

'And it still hasn't come back to you?' asked Ninian, delicately sympathetic towards the old and forgetful.

'It has not. Not even here. Have you fared any better?'

'It was a thin hope to find what I came for,' said Ninian ruefully, 'though I did risk coming before the light was quite gone. But at least I know what I came looking for. I was there with Diota when you brought him back on Christmas Day, and I never thought what was missing until later. After all, it's a thing that could well go astray, not like the clothes

136

he was wearing. But I knew he had it with him when he came stamping along the path and stabbing at the ground. Coming all this way through England in his company, I got to know it very well. That great staff he was always so lungeous with – ebony, tall as his elbow, with a stag's-horn handle – that's what I came to look for. And somewhere here it must still be.'

They had emerged on to the low shore, dappled now with moist dark patches of grass breaking through the tattered snow. The dull, pale level of the water stretched away to the dark slope of the further bank. Cadfael had stopped abruptly, staring over the shield of pallor in startled enlightenment.

'So it must!' he said devoutly. 'So it must! Child, that's the will-o'-the-wisp I've been chasing all this day. You get back to your refuge and keep snug within, and leave this search to me now. You've read my riddle for me.'

By morning half the snow had melted and vanished, and the Foregate was like a coil of tattered and threadbare lace. The cobbles of the great court shone moist and dark, and in the graveyard east of the church Cynric had broken the turf for Father Ailnoth's grave.

Cadfael came from the last chapter of the year with a strong feeling that more things than the year were ending. No word had yet been said of who was to succeed to the living of Holy Cross, no word would be said until Ailnoth was safely under the ground, with every proper rite and as much mourning as brotherhood and parish could muster between them. The next day, the birth of another year, would see the burial of a brief tyranny that would soon be gratefully forgotten. God send us, thought Cadfael, a humble soul who thinks himself as fallible as his flock, and labours modestly to keep both from falling. If two hold fast together they stand steadily, but if one holds aloof the other may find his feet betraying him in slippery places. Better a limping prop than a solid rock for ever out of reach of the stretched hand.

Cadfael made for the wicket in the wall, and went through to the shores of the mill-pond. He stood on the edge of the overhanging bank between the pollarded willows, at the spot where he had found Ailnoth's body, the pool widening and shallowing on his right hand into the reed beds below the highway, and on his left gradually narrowing to the deeper stream that carried the water back to the brook, and shortly thereafter to the Severn. The body had entered the water probably a few yards to the right, and been nudged aside here under the bank by the tail-race. The skull-cap had been found in the reeds, somewhere accessible from the path on the opposite side. A small, light thing, it would go with the current until reeds or branch or debris in the water arrested it. But where would a heavy ebony staff be carried, whether it flew from his hand as he was struck down, or whether it was thrown in after him, from this spot? It would either be drifted aside in the same direction as the body, in which case it might be sunk deep somewhere in the narrowing channel, or else, if it fell on the other side of the main force of the tail-race, edged away like the skull-cap into the far shore. At least there was no harm in circling the shallow bowl and looking for it.

He re-crossed the little bridge over the head-race, circled the mill and went down to the edge of the water. There was no real path here, the gardens of the three small houses came almost to the lip of the bank, where a narrow strip of open grass just allowed of passage. For some way the path was still raised above water level, and somewhat hollowed out beneath, then it dropped gradually into the first growth of reeds, and he walked in tufted grass, with moisture welling round every step he took. Under the miller's house and garden, under the house where the deaf old woman lived with her pretty slattern of a maidservant, and then he was bearing somewhat away from the final house, round the rim of the broad shallows. Silver of water gleamed through the blanched, pallid green of winter reeds, but though an accumulation of leaves, dead twigs and branches had drifted

138

and lodged here, he saw no sign of an ebony walking-staff. Other cast-offs, however, showed themselves, broken crockery, discarded shards and a holed pot, too far gone to be worth mending.

He went on, round the broad end of the pool, to the trickle of water that came down from the conduit under the highway, stepped over that, and on beneath the gardens of the second trio of abbey houses. Somewhere here the boys had found the cap, but he could not believe he would find the staff here. Either he had missed it, or, if it had been flung well out over the drift of the tail-race, he must look for it on the far side of the channel opposite where the body had been found. The water was still fairly wide there, but what fell beyond its centre might well fetch up on this far side.

He halted to consider, glad he had put on boots to wade about this thawing quagmire. His friend and fellow Welshman, Madog of the Dead Boat, who knew everything there was to be known about water and its properties, given an idea of the thing sought, could have told him exactly where to seek it. But Madog was not here, and time was precious, and he must manage on his own. Ebony was heavy and solid, but still it was wood, and would float. Nor would it float evenly, having a stag's-horn handle, a tip should break the surface, wherever it lodged, and he did not believe it would be carried so far as the brook and the river. Doggedly he went on, and on this side the water there was a trodden path, which gradually lifted out of the boggy ground, and carried him dry-shod a little above the surface of the pool.

He drew level with the mill opposite, and was past the sloping strips of garden on this side the water. The stunted willow stump, defiantly sprouting its head of startled hair, matched his progress and held his eye. Just beyond that the body had lain, nuzzling the undercut bank.

Three paces more, and he found what he was seeking. Barely visible through the fringe of rotting ice and the protruding ends of grass, only its tip emerging, Ailnoth's staff lay at his feet. He took it gingerly by its tapered end, and plucked it out of the water. No mistaking it, once found, there could hardly be two exactly alike. Black and long, with a metal-shod tip and a grooved horn handle, banded to the shaft by a worn silver band embossed in some pattern worn very smooth with age. Whether flying out of the victim's hand or thrown in afterwards, it must have fallen into the water on this side of the current's main flow, and so been cast up here into the encroaching border of grass.

Melting snow dripped from the handle and ran down the shaft. Carrying it by the middle of the shaft, Cadfael turned back on his tracks, and circled the reedy shallows back to the mill. He was not yet ready to share his prize with anyone, not even Hugh, until he had had a close look at it, and extracted from it whatever it had to tell him. His hopes were not high, but he could not afford to let any hint slip through his fingers. He hurried through the wicket in the precinct wall, and across the great court, and went to earth in his own workshop. He left the door open for the sake of light, but also lit a wooden spill at the brazier and kindled his little lamp to make a close examination of the trophy.

The hand-long piece of horn, pale brown furrowed with wavy ruts of darker brown, was heavy and polished from years of use, and its slight curve fitted well into the hand. The band of silver was a thumb-joint wide, and the half-eroded vine leaves with which it was engraved reflected the yellow light of the lamp from worn highlights as Cadfael carefully dabbed off the moisture and held it close to the flame. The silver had worn thin as gauze, and grown so pliant to every touch that both rims had frayed up into rough edges here and there, sharp as knife blades. Cadfael had scratched a finger in drying the metal before he realised the danger.

This was the formidable weapon with which Father Ailnoth had lashed out at the vexatious urchins who played games against the wall of his house, and no doubt prodded the ribs or thumped the shoulders of the unlucky pupils who were less than perfect in their lessons. Cadfael turned it slowly in his hands in the close light of the lamp, and shook

140

his head over the sins of the virtuous. It was while he was so turning it that his eye was caught by the brief, passing gleam of a drop of moisture, spinning past an inch or more from the rim of silver. Hastily he checked, and turned the staff counterwise, and the bead of brightness reappeared. A single minute drop, clinging not to the metal, but to a fine thread held by the metal, something that appeared and vanished in a silvery curve. He uncoiled on his finger-end a long, greying hair, drawing it forth until it resisted, caught in a sharp edge of silver. Not one hair only, for now a second was partly drawn forth with it, and a third made a small, tight ring, stuck fast in the same tiny nick.

It took him some little time to detach them all from the notch in the lower rim of the band, five of them in all, as well as a few tangled ends. The five were all of fine hair, some brown, some greying to silver, and long, too long for any tonsure, too long for a man, unless he wore his hair neglected and untrimmed. If there had ever been any further mark, of blood, or grazed skin, or thread from a cloth, the water had soaked it away, but these hairs, caught fast in the worn metal, had held their place, to give up their testimony at last.

Cadfael ran a careful hand up the shaft of the staff, and felt the needle-stabs of three or four rough points in the silver. In the deepest of these five precious hairs had been dragged by violence from a head. A woman's head!

Diota opened the door to him, and on recognising her visitor seemed to hesitate whether to open it wider and step aside to let him in, or hold her ground and discourage any lengthy conversation by keeping him on the doorstep. Her face was guarded and still, and her greeting resigned rather than welcoming. But the hesitation was only momentary. Submissively she stepped back into the room, and Cadfael followed her within and closed the door upon the world. It was early afternoon, the light as good as it would be this day, and the fire in the clay hearth bright and clear, almost without smoke.

'Mistress Hammet,' said Cadfael, with no more than a yard of dim, warm air between their faces, 'I must talk with you, and what I have to say concerns also the welfare of Ninian Bachiler, whom I know you value. I am in his confidence, if that helps me to yours. Now sit, and listen to me, and believe in my goodwill, as you have nothing on your conscience but the heart's affection. Which God saw clearly, before ever I held a key to it.'

She turned from him abruptly, but with a suggestion rather of balance and resolution than shock and dread, and sat down on the bench where Sanan had been sitting on his former visit. She sat erect, drawn up with elbows tight at her sides and feet firmly planted.

'Do you know where he is?' she asked in a low voice.

'I do not, though he made to tell me. Rest easy, I talked with him only last night, I know he is well. What I have to say has to do with you, and with what happened on the eve of the Nativity, when Father Ailnoth died, and you . . . had a fall on the ice.'

She was already certain that he had knowledge she had hoped to keep from the light, but she did not know what it was. She kept silence, her eyes lifted steadily to his face, and left it to him to continue.

'A fall – yes! You won't have forgotten. You fell on the icy road and struck your head on the doorstone. I dressed the wound then, I saw it again yesterday, and it has healed over, but it still shows the bruise, and the scar where the skin was broken. Now hear what I have found this morning, in the mill-pond. Father Ailnoth's staff, drifted across to the far shore, and caught in the worn silver band, where the thin edges have turned, and are rough and sharp, five long hairs, the like of yours. Yours I saw closely, when I bathed your wound, I know there were broken ends there. I have the means to match them now.'

She had sunk her head into her hands, the long, work-worn fingers clutched cheek and temple hard.

'Why should you hide your face?' he said temperately.

'That was not your sin.'

In a little while she raised a tearless face, blanched and wary, and peered at him steadily between her supporting hands. 'I was here,' she said slowly, 'when the nobleman came. I knew him again, I knew why he was here. Why else should he come?'

'Why, indeed! And when he was gone, the priest turned upon you. Reviled you, perhaps cursed you, for an accomplice in treason, for a liar and deceiver. . . . We have learned to know him well enough to know that he would not be merciful, nor listen to excuse or pleading. Did he threaten you? Tell you how he would crush your nurseling first, and discard you with ignominy afterwards?'

Her back stiffened. She said with dignity: 'I nursed my lamb at this breast after my own child was born dead. He had a sickly mother, poor sweet lady. When he came to me, it was as if a son of my own had come home in need. Do you think I cared what he – my master – might do against me?'

'No, I believe you,' said Cadfael. 'Your thought was all of Ninian when you went out after Father Ailnoth that night, to try to turn him from his purpose of challenge and betrayal. For you did follow him, did you not? You must have followed him. How else have I teased your hairs out of the worn band of his staff? You followed and pleaded with him, and he struck you. Clubbed his staff and struck out at your head.'

'I clung to him,' she said, with stony calm now, 'fell on my knees in the frosty grass there by the mill, and clung to the skirts of his gown to hold him, and would not let go. I prayed him, I pleaded, I begged him for mercy, but he had none. Yes, he struck me. He could not endure to be so held and crossed, it enraged him, he might well have killed me. Or so I dreaded then. I tried to fend off his blows, but I knew he would strike again if he could not rid himself of me. So I loosed hold and got to my feet, God knows how, and ran from him. And that was the last I ever saw of him living.'

'And you neither saw nor heard any other creature there?

You left him whole, and alone?'

'I tell you truth,' she said, shaking her head, 'I neither heard nor saw any other soul, not even when I reached the Foregate. But neither my eyes nor my ears were clear, my head so rang, and I was in such sick despair. The first I was truly aware of was blood running down my forehead, and then I was in this house, crouched on the floor by the hearth, and shivering with the cold of fear, with no notion how I got here. I ran like an animal to its den, and that was all I knew. Only I am sure I met no one on the way, because if I had I should have had to master myself, walk like a woman in her senses, even give a greeting. And when you have to, you can. No, I know nothing more after I fled from him. All night I waited in fear of his return, knowing he would not spare me, and dreading he had already done his worst against Ninian. I was sure then that we were both lost – that everything was lost.'

'But he did not come,' said Cadfael.

'No, he did not come. I bathed my head, and stanched the blood, and waited without hope, but he never came. It was no help to me. Fear of him turned about into fear for him, for what could he be doing, out in the frost all night long? Even if he had gone up to the castle and called out the guard there, still it could not have kept him so long. But he didn't come. Think for yourself what manner of night I spent, sleepless in his house, waiting.'

'There was also, perhaps worst of all,' said Cadfael gently, 'your fear that he had indeed met with Ninian at the mill after you fled, and come to grief at Ninian's hands.'

She said, 'Yes,' in a dry whisper, and shivered. 'It could have been so. A boy of such spirit, challenged, accused, perhaps attacked. . . . It could have been so. Thanks be to God, it was not so!'

'And in the morning? You could not leave it longer or leave it to others to raise an alarm. So you came to the church.'

'And told half a story,' she said with a brief, twisted smile, like a contortion of pain. 'What else could I do?'

'And while we went searching for the priest, Ninian stayed with you, and told you, doubtless, how he had spent the night, knowing nothing at all of what had happened after he left the mill. As doubtless you told him the rest of your story. But neither of you could shed light on the man's death.'

'That is true,' said Diota, 'I swear it. Neither then nor now. And now what do you intend for me?'

'Why, simply that you should do what Abbot Radulfus charged you, continue here and keep this house in readiness for another priest, and trust his word that you shall not be abandoned, since the church brought you here. I must be free to make use of what I know, but it shall be done with as little harm to you as possible, and only when I have understood more than now I understand. I wish you could have helped me one more step on the road, but never mind, truth is there to be found, and there must be a way to it. There were three people, besides Ailnoth, went to the mill that night,' said Cadfael, pausing at the door. 'Ninian was the first, you were the second. I wonder – I wonder! – who was the third?'

Chapter Ten

Cadfael had been back in his workshop no more than half an hour, and the light was only just beginning to dim towards the Vesper office, when Hugh came seeking him, as he usually did if shire affairs brought him to confer with the abbot. He brought in with him a gust of moist, chill air and the quiver of a rising breeze that might bring more snow, now that the hard frost had eased, or might blow away the heavy cloud and clear the sky for the morrow.

'I've been with Father Abbot,' said Hugh, and sat down on the familiar bench by the wall and spread his feet appreciatively towards the brazier. 'Tomorrow, I hear, you're burying the priest. Cynric has the grave dug for him so deep you'd think he feared the man might break out of it without six feet of earth on top of him to hold him down. Well, he's going to his funeral unavenged, for we're no nearer knowing who killed him. You said from the first that the entire Foregate would turn blind, deaf and dumb. A man would think the whole parish had been depeopled on Christmas Eve, no one will admit to having been out of his own house but to hurry to church, and not a man of them set eyes on any other living being in the streets that night. It took a stranger to let fall even one little word of furtive comings and goings at an ungodly hour, and I place no great credence in that. And how have you been faring?'

Cadfael had been wondering the same thing in his own mind ever since leaving Diota, and could see no possibility of keeping back from Hugh what he had learned. He had not promised secrecy, only discretion, and he owed help to Hugh as surely as to the woman caught in the trap of her own devotion.

'Better, perhaps, than I deserve,' he said sombrely, and put aside the tray of tablets he had just set out to dry, and went to sit beside his friend. 'If you had not come to me, Hugh, I should have had to come to you. Last night it was brought back to me what I had seen in Ailnoth's possession that night, and had not found nor thought to look for again the next day, when we brought him back here dead. Two things, indeed, though the first I did not find myself, but got it from the little boys who went down hopefully to the pool on Christmas morning, thinking it might be frozen over. Wait a moment, I'll bring both, and you shall hear.'

He brought them, and carried the lamp closer, to show the detail that might mean so much or so little.

'This cap the children found among the reeds of the shallows. You see how the stitches are started in the one seam, and the binding ripped loose. And this staff – this I found only this morning, almost opposite the place where we found Ailnoth.' He told that story simply and truthfully, but for omitting any mention of Ninian, though that, too, might have to come. 'You see how the silver band is worn into a mere wafer from age, and crumpled at the edges, being so thin. This notch here. . .' He set a finger-tip to the razor-sharp points. 'From this I wormed out *these!*'

He had dabbed a tiny spot of grease into one of his clay saucers for selecting seed, and anchored the rescued hairs to the congealed fat, so that no chance draught should blow them away. In the close yellow light of the lamp they showed clearly. Cadfael drew out one of them to its full length.

'A metal edge fissured like this might pick up a stray hair almost anywhere,' said Hugh, but not with any great conviction.

'So it might, but here are five, captured at the same mis-stroke. Which makes this a different matter. Well?'

Hugh likewise laid a finger to the glistening threads and said deliberately: 'A woman's. Not young.'

'Whether you yet know it or no,' said Cadfael, 'there are but two women in all this coil, and one of them is young, and will not be grey, please God, for many years yet.'

'I think,' said Hugh, eyeing him with a faint, wise smile, 'you had better tell me. You were here from the beginning, I came late, and brought with me another matter warranted to confuse the first. I am not interested in preventing young Bachiler from making clean away to Gloucester to fight for his Empress, if he has nothing on his conscience that chances to be more particularly my business. But I *am* interested in burying the ugly fact of murder along with Ailnoth tomorrow, if by any means I can. I want the town and the Foregate going about their day's work with a quiet mind, and the way cleared for another priest, and let's hope one easier to live with. Now, what I make of these hairs is that they came from the head of Dame Diota Hammet. I have not even seen the woman in a good light, to know if this colouring is hers, but even there indoors the bruise on her brow was plain to be seen. She had a fall on the icy step – so I had been told, and so she told me. I think you are saying she came by that injury in a very different manner.'

'She came by it,' said Cadfael, 'by the mill that night, when she followed the priest in desperation, to plead with him to let well alone and turn a blind eye to the boy's deception, instead of confronting him like an avenging demon and fetching your sergeants down on him to throw him into prison. She was Ninian's nurse, she would dare almost anything for his sake. She clung about Ailnoth's skirts and begged him to let be, and because he could not shake her off, he clubbed this staff of his and struck her on the head, and would have struck again if she had not loosed him and scrambled away half-stunned, and run for her life back to the house.'

He told the whole of it as he had had it from Diota herself, and Hugh listened with a grave face but the hint of the smile lingering thoughtfully in his eyes. 'You believe this,' he said at the end of it; not a question, but a fact, and relevant to his own thinking.

'I do believe it. Entirely.'

'And she can add nothing more, to point us to any other person. Or would she, even if she could?' wondered Hugh. 'She may very well feel with the Foregate, and prefer to keep her own counsel.'

'So she might, I won't deny, but for all that, I think she knows no more. She ran from him dazed and in terror. I think there's no more to be got from her.'

'Nor from your boy Benet?' said Hugh slyly, and laughed at seeing Cadfael turn a sharp glance on him and bridle for a moment. 'Oh, come now, I do accept that it was not you who warned the boy to make himself scarce when Giffard brought the law down on him. But only because someone else had already spared you the trouble. You were very well aware that he was gone, when you so helpfully led us all round the garden here hunting for him. I'll even believe that you *had* seen him here not half an hour before. You have a way of telling simple truths which is anything but simple. And when did you ever have a young fellow in trouble under your eye, and not wind your way into his confidence? Of course he'll have opened his mind to you. I daresay you know where he is this very moment. Though I'm not asking!' he added hastily.

'No,' said Cadfael, well satisfied with the way that was phrased, 'no, that I don't know, so you may ask, for I can't tell you.'

'Having gone to some trouble not to find out or be told,' agreed Hugh, grinning. 'Well, I did tell you to keep him out of sight if you should happen on him. I might even turn a blind eye myself, once this other matter is cleared up.'

'As to that,' said Cadfael candidly, 'he's of the same mind as you, for until he knows that all's made plain, and Dame Hammet safe and respected, he won't budge. Much as he wants to get to honest service in Gloucester, here he stays while she's in trouble. Which is only fair, seeing the risks she has taken for him. But once this is over, he'll be away, out of your territory. And not alone!' said Cadfael, meeting Hugh's quizzical glance with a complacent countenance. 'Is it possible I still know something you do not know?'

Hugh furrowed his brow and considered this riddle at leisure. 'Not Giffard, that's certain! He could not get himself out of the trap fast enough. Two women in the affair, you said, one of them young. . . . Do you tell me this young venturer has found himself a wife in these parts? Already? These imps of Anjou work briskly, I grant them that! Let's see, then. . . .' He pondered, drumming his fingers thoughtfully on the rim of the clay saucer. 'He had got himself into a monastery, where women do not abound, and I think you will have got your due of work out of him, he had small opportunity to go wooing among the townswomen. And as far as I know, he made no approach to any other of the local lordlings. I'm left with Giffard's household, where the boy's embassage may have been a none too well-kept secret, and where there's a very pleasing young woman, of the Empress's faction by blood, and bold and determined enough to choose differently from her step-father. Why, pure curiosity would have brought her to have a close look at such a paladin of romance, come in peril of his liberty and life from over the sea. Sanan Bernières? Is he truly wanting to take her with him?'

'Sanan it is. But I think it was she who made the decision. They have horses hidden away ready for departure, and she has her own small estate in jewels from her mother, easily carried. No doubt she's provided him sword and dagger, too. She'll not let him come before the Empress or Robert of Gloucester shabby, or without arms and horse.'

'They mean this earnestly?' wondered Hugh, frowning over a private doubt as to what his own course ought to be in such a case.

'They mean it. Both of them. I doubt if Giffard will mind much, though he's done his duty by her fairly enough. It saves him a dowry. And the man's had his losses, and is ambitious for his son.'

'And what,' demanded Hugh, 'does she get out of it?'

'She gets her own way. She gets what she wants, and the man she's chosen for herself. She gets Ninian. I think it may not be a bad bargain.'

Hugh sat silent for a brooding while, weighing the rights and wrongs of allowing such a flight, and recalling, perhaps, his own determined pursuit of Aline, not so long past. After a while his brow smoothed, and the private gleam of mischief quickened in his black eyes and twitched at the corner of his mouth. An eloquent eyebrow tilted above a covert glance at Cadfael.

'Well, I can as easily put a stop to that as cross the court here, yes, and bring the lad flying out of hiding into my arms, if I choose. You've taught me the way to flush him out of cover. All I need do is arrest Mistress Hammet, or even put it abroad that I'm about to, and he'll come running to defend her. If I accused her of murder, as like as not he'd go so far as to confess to an act he never committed, to see her free and vindicated.'

'You could do it,' Cadfael admitted, without any great concern, 'but you won't. You are as convinced as I am that neither he nor Dame Diota ever laid hand on Ailnoth, and you certainly won't pretend otherwise.'

'I might, however,' said Hugh, grinning, 'try the same trick with another victim, and see if the man who did drown Ailnoth will be as honest and chivalrous as your lad would be. For I came here today with a small item of news you will not yet have heard, concerning one of Ailnoth's flock who'll be none the worse for a salutary shock. Who knows, there are plenty of rough and ready fellows who would kill lightly enough, but not stand by and let another man be hanged for it. It would be worth the trial, to hook a murderer, and even if it failed, the bait would come to no lasting harm.'

'I would not do it to a dog!' said Cadfael.

'Neither would I, dogs are honest, worthy creatures that fight fair and bear no grudges. When they set out to kill, they do it openly in broad daylight, and never care how many witnesses there may be. I have less scruples about some men.

This one – ah, he's none so bad, but a fright won't hurt him, and may do a very sound turn for his poor drab of a wife.'

'You have lost me,' said Cadfael.

'Let me find you again! This morning Alan Herbard brought me a man he'd happened on by chance, a country kinsman of Erwald's who came to spend Christmas with the provost and his family here in the Foregate. The man's a shepherd by calling, and Erwald had a couple of ewes too early in lamb, penned in his shed out beyond the Gaye, and one of them threatened to cast her lamb too soon. So his cousin the shepherd went to the shed after Matins and Lauds on Christmas morning, to take a look at them, and brought off the threatened lamb safely, too, and was on his way back, just coming up from the Gaye and along to the Foregate at first light. And who do you suppose he saw sneaking very furtively up from the path to the mill and heading for home, but Jordan Achard, rumpled and bleared from sleep and hardly expecting to be seen at that hour. By chance one of the few people our man would have known by sight and name here, being the baker from whose oven he'd fetched his cousin's bread the day before. It came out in purest gossip, in all innocence. The countryman knew Jordan's reputation, and thought it a harmless joke to have seen him making for home from some strange bed.'

'Along that path?' said Cadfael, staring.

'Along that path. It was well trodden that night, it seems.'

'Ninian was the first,' said Cadfael slowly. 'I never told you that, but he went there early, not being sure of Giffard. He took himself off smartly when he saw Ailnoth come raging to the meeting, and nothing more did he know of it until morning, when Diota came crying the priest was lost. She was there, as I've told you. I said there must be a third. But Jordan? And blundering homeward at first light? It's hard to believe he had so much durable malice in him as to carry his grudge so long. A big, spoiled babe, I should have said, but for being an excellent baker.'

'So should I. But he was there, no question. Who's abroad

152

at first light on Christmas morning, after a long night's worship? Barring, of course, a shepherd anxious about an ailing ewe! That was very ill luck for Jordan. But it goes further, Cadfael. I went myself to talk to Jordan's wife, while he was busy at his ovens. I told her what news we had of his moves, and made her understand it was proven beyond doubt where he'd been. I think she was ready to break like a branch over-fruited. Do you know how many children she's borne, poor soul? Eleven, and only two of them living. And how he managed to engender so many, considering how seldom he lies at home, only the recording angel can tell. Not a bad-looking woman, if she were not so worn and harried. And still fond of him!'

'And this time,' said Cadfael, awed, 'she really told you truth?'

'Of course she did, she was rightly afraid for him. Yes, she told truth. Yes, he was out all that night, it was nothing new. But not murdering anyone! No, on that she was insistent, he would not hurt a fly. He's done his worst by a poor wretch of a wife, however! All he'd been about, she said, was bedding his latest fancy girl, and that was the bold little bitch who's maidservant to the old woman who lives next to the miller, by the pool.'

'Ah, now that's a far more likely thing,' said Cadfael, enlightened. 'That rings true! We talked to her,' he recalled, fascinated, 'next morning, when we were looking for Ailnoth.' A pretty slut of about eighteen, with a mane of dark hair and bold, inquisitive eyes, saying: 'Not a soul that I know of came along here in the night, why should they?' No, she had not been lying. She had never thought of her covert lover as counting among the furtive visitors to the mill in the darkness. His errand was known, and if not innocent, entirely natural and harmless. She spoke according to her understanding.

'And she never said word of Jordan! No, why should she? She knew what he'd been up to, it was not about him you were asking. Oh, no, I've nothing against the girl. But I would stake much that she knows nothing of time, and has no notion exactly when he came or when he left, except by the beginning of light. He could have killed a man before ever he whispered at the deaf woman's door, for ears that were forewarned and sharp enough.'

'I doubt if he did,' said Cadfael.

'So do I. But see how beautiful a case I can make against him! His wife has admitted that he went there. The shepherd saw him leaving. We know that Father Ailnoth went along that same path. After Mistress Hammet had fled from him, still he waited for his prey. And how if he saw a parishioner of his, already in dispute with him, and whose reputation he may well have heard before then, whispering his way furtively into a strange house, and being let in by a young woman? How then? His nose was expert at detecting sinners, he might well be distracted from his first purpose to flush out an evil-doer on the spot. The old woman is stone deaf. The girl, if she witnessed such a collision, and saw its end, would hold her tongue and tell a good story. In such a case, Cadfael, old friend, the priest might well have started too hot a hare, and got the worst of it, ending in the pool.'

'The blow to Ailnoth's head,' said Cadfael, jolted, 'was deep to the back. Men in conflict go face to face.'

'True, but one may easily be spun aside and involuntarily turn his back for an instant. But you know how the wound lay, and I know. But do the commons know?'

'And you will really do this?' marvelled Cadfael.

'Most publicly, my friend, I will do it. Tomorrow morning, at Ailnoth's funeral – even those who most hated him will be there to make sure he's safely underground, what better occasion could there be? If it bears fruit, then we have our answer, and the town can be at peace, once the turmoil's over. If not, Jordan will be none the worse for a short-lived fright, and a few nights, perhaps,' pondered Hugh, gleaming mischief, 'on a harder bed than usual with him, and lying alone. He may even learn that his own bed is the safest from this on.'

154

'And how if no man speaks up to deliver him,' said Cadfael with mild malice, 'and the thing happened just as you have pictured it to me a minute ago, and Jordan really is your man? What then? If he keep his head and deny all, and the girl bears witness for him, you'll have trailed your bait in vain.'

'Ah, you know the man better than that,' said Hugh, undisturbed. 'Big-boned and hearty, but no great stiffening in his back. If he did it, deny it as loudly as he may when he's first accused, a couple of nights on stone and he'll be blabbing out everything, how he did no more than defend himself, how it was mere accident, and he could not haul the priest out of the water, and took fright, and dared not speak, knowing that the bad blood between them was common knowledge. A couple of nights in a cell won't hurt him. And if he holds out stoutly any longer than that,' said Hugh, rising, 'then he deserves to get away with it. The parish will think so.'

'You are a devious creature,' said Cadfael, in a tone uncertain between reproach and admiration. 'I wonder why I bear with you?'

Hugh turned in the doorway to give him a flashing glance over his shoulder. 'Like calling to like, I daresay!' he suggested, and went striding away along the gravel path, to disappear into the gathering dusk.

At Vespers the psalms had a penitential solemnity, and at Collations in the chapter house after supper the readings were also of a funereal colouring. The shadow of Father Ailnoth hung over the death of the year, and it seemed that the year of Our Lord 1142 would be born, not at midnight, but only after the burial service was over, and the grave filled in. The morrow might, according to the Church's calendar, be the octave of the Nativity and the celebration of the Circumcision of Our Lord, but to the people of the Foregate it was rather the propitiatory office that would lift their incubus from them. A wretched departure for any man, let alone a priest.

'On the morrow,' said Prior Robert, before dismissing them to the warming room for the blessed last half-hour of ease before Compline, 'the funeral office for Father Ailnoth will follow immediately after the parish Mass, and I myself shall preside. But the homily will be delivered by Father Abbot, at his desire.' The prior's incisive and well-modulated voice made this statement with a somewhat ambiguous emphasis, as if in doubt whether to welcome the abbot's decision as a devout compliment to the dead, or to regret and perhaps even resent it as depriving him of an opportunity to exercise his own undoubted eloquence. 'Matins and Lauds will be said according to the Office of the Dead.'

That meant that they would be long, and prudent brothers would be wise to make straight for their beds after Compline. Cadfael had already turfed down his brazier to burn slowly through the night, and keep lotions and medicines from freezing and bottles from bursting, should a hard frost set in again in the small hours. But the air was certainly not cold enough yet for frost, and he thought by the slight wind and lightly overcast sky that they would get through the night safely. He went thankfully to the warming room with his brothers, and settled down to half an hour of pleasant idleness.

This was the hour when even the taciturn relaxed into speech, and not even the prior frowned upon a degree of loquacity. And inevitably the subject of their exchanges tonight was the brief rule of Father Ailnoth, his grim death, and the coming ceremonial of his burial.

'So Father Abbot means to pronounce the eulogy himself, does he?' said Brother Anselm in Cadfael's ear. 'That will make interesting listening.' Anselm's business was the music of the Divine Office, and he had not quite the same regard for the spoken word, but he appreciated its power and influence. 'I had thought he'd be only too glad to leave it to Robert. *Nil nisi bonum*. . . . Or do you suppose he looks upon it as a fitting penance for bringing the man here in the first place?'

'There may be something in that,' admitted Cadfael. 'But

more, I think, in a resolve that only truth shall be told. Robert would be carried away into paeans of praise. Radulfus intends clarity and honesty.'

'No easy task,' said Anselm. 'Well for me no one expects words from me. There's been no hint yet of who's to follow in the parish. They'll be praying for a man they know, whether he has any Latin or not. Even a man they did not much like would be welcomed, if he belongs here, and knows them. You can deal with the devil you know.'

'No harm in hoping for better than that,' said Cadfael, sighing. 'A very ordinary man, more than a little lower than the angels, and well aware of his own shortcomings, would do very nicely for the Foregate. A pity these few weeks were wasted, wanting him.'

In the big stone hearth the fire of logs burned steadily, sinking down now into a hot core of ash, nicely timed to last the evening out, and die down with little waste when the bell rang for Compline. Faces pinched with cold and outdoor labour during the day flushed into rosy content, and chapped hands smoothed gratefully at the ointment doled out from Cadfael's store. Friends foregathered in their own chosen groups, voices decorously low blended into a contented murmur like a hive of bees. Some of the healthy young, who had been out in the air most of the day, had much ado to keep their eyelids open in the warmth. Compline would be wisely brief tonight, as Matins would be long and sombre.

'Another year tomorrow,' said Brother Edmund the infirmarer, 'and a new beginning.'

Some said: 'Amen!' whether from habit or conviction, but Cadfael stuck fast at the word. 'Amen' belongs rather to an ending, a resolution, an acceptance into peace, and as yet they were within reach of none of these things.

A mile to the west of Cadfael's bed in his narrow cell in the dortoir, Ninian lay in the plenteous hay of a well-stocked loft, rolled in the cloak Sanan had brought for him, and with the heartening warmth of her still in his arms, though she had been gone two hours and more, in time to have her pony back in the town stable before her step-father returned from the night office at Saint Chad's church. Ninian had been urgent with her that she should not venture alone by night, but as yet he had no authority over her, and she would do what she would do, having been born into the world apparently without fear. This byre and loft on the edge of the forest belonged to the Giffards, who had grazing along the open meadow that rimmed the trees, but the elderly hind who kept the cattle was from Sanan's own household, and her willing and devoted slave. The two good horses she had bought and stabled here were his joy, and his privity to Sanan's marriage plans would keep him proud and glad to the day of his death.

She had come, and she had lain with Ninian in the loft, the two rolled in one cloak and anchored with embracing arms, not yet for the body's delight but rather for its survival and comfort. Snug like dormice in their winter sleep, alive and awake enough to be aware of profound pleasure, they had talked together almost an hour, and now that she had left him he hugged the remembrance of her and got warmth from it to keep him glowing through the night. Some day, some night, please God soon, she would not have to rise and leave him, he would not have to open reluctant arms and let her go, and the night would be perfect, a lovely, starry dark shot through with flame. But now he lay alone, and ached a little, and fretted about her, about the morrow, about his own debts, which seemed to him so inadequately paid.

With her hair adrift against his cheek, and her breath warm in the hollow of his throat, she had told him everything that had happened during these last days of the old year, how Brother Cadfael had found the ebony staff, how he had visited Diota and got her story out of her, how Father Ailnoth's funeral was to take place next day after the parish Mass. And when he started up in anxiety for Diota, she had drawn him down to her again with her arms wreathed about his neck, and told him he need have no uneasiness, for she had promised to go with Diota to the priest's funeral Mass, and take as great care of her as he himself could have done, and deal with any threat that might arise against her as valiantly as even he would have dealt with it. And she had forbidden him to stir from where he lay hidden until she should come to him again. But just as she was a lady not lightly to be disobeyed, so he was a man not lightly to be forbidden.

All the same, she had got a promise out of him that he would wait, as she insisted, unless something unforeseen should arise to make action imperative. And with that she had had to be content, and they had kissed on it, and put away present anxieties to whisper about the future. How many miles to the Welsh border? Ten? Certainly not much more. And Powys might be a wild land, but it had no quarrel with a soldier of the Empress more than with an officer of King Stephen, and would by instinct take the part of the hunted rather than the forces of English law. Moreover, Sanan had claims to a distant kinship there, through a Welsh grandmother, who had bequeathed her her un-English name. And should they encounter masterless men in the forests, Ninian was a good man of his hands, and there was a good sword and a long dagger hidden away in the hay, arms once carried by John Bernières at the siege of Shrewsbury, where he had met his death. They would do well enough on the journey, they would reach Gloucester and marry there, openly and honourably.

Except that they could not go, not yet, not until he was satisfied that all danger to Diota was past, and her living secure under the abbot's protection. And now that he lay alone, Ninian could see no present end to that difficulty. The morrow would lay Ailnoth's body to rest, but not the ugly shadow of his death. Even if the day passed without threat to Diota, that would not solve anything for the days yet to come.

Ninian lay wakeful until past midnight, fretting at the threads that would not untangle for him. Over the watershed between the old year and the new he drifted at last into an uneasy sleep, and dreamed of fighting his way through interminable forest tracks overgrown with bramble and thorn towards a Sanan forever withdrawn from him, and leaving behind for him only a sweet, aromatic scent of herbs.

Under the vast inverted keel of the choir, dimly lit for Matins, the solemn words of the Office of the Dead echoed and re-echoed as sounds never seemed to do by day, and the fine, sonorous voice of Brother Benedict the sacristan was magnified to fill the whole vault as he read the lessons in between the spoken psalms, and at every ending came the insistent versicle and response:

'*Requiem aeternam dona eis, Domine.* . . .'
'*Et lux perpetua luceat eis.* . . .'

And Brother Benedict, deep and splendid: ' "My soul is weary of my life. . . . I will speak in the bitterness of my soul, I will say unto God, Do not condemn me, show me wherefore thou contendest with me. . . ." '

Not much comfort in the book of Job, thought Cadfael, listening intently in his stall, but a great deal of fine poetry – could not that in itself be a kind of comfort, after all? Making even discomfort, degradation and death, everything Job complained of, a magnificent defiance?

'"O that thou wouldst hide me in the grave, that thou wouldst keep me secret until thy wrath be past. . . .

'"My breath is corrupt, my days are extinct, the grave is ready for me. . . . I have made my bed in the darkness, I have said to corruption, Thou art my father, to the worm, Thou art my mother. And where is now my hope?

'"Cease, then, and let me alone, that I may take comfort a little, before I go whence I shall not return, even to the land of darkness and the shadow of death . . . land without order, where even the light is as darkness. . . ."'

Yet in the end the entreaty that was itself a reassurance rose again, one step advanced beyond hope towards certainty:

'*Rest eternal grant unto them, O Lord.* . . .'

'And let light perpetual shine upon them. . . .'

Stumbling up the night stairs back to bed after Lauds, half asleep, Cadfael still had that persistent appeal echoing in his mind, and by the time he slept again it had become almost a triumphant claim reaching up to take what it pleaded for. Rest eternal and light perpetual . . . even for Ailnoth.

Not only for Ailnoth, but for most of us, thought Cadfael, subsiding into sleep, it will be a long journey through purgatory, but no doubt even the most winding way gets there in the end.

Chapter Eleven

The first day of the New Year, 1142, dawned grey and moist, but with a veiled light that suggested the sun might come through slowly, and abide for an hour or so in the middle of the day, before mist again closed in towards nightfall. Cadfael, who was often up well before Prime, awakened this morning only when the bell sounded, and made his way down the night stairs with the others still drowsy from so short a rest. After Prime he went to make sure that all was well in the workshop, and brought away with him fresh oil for the altar lamps. Cynric had already trimmed the candles, and gone out through the cloister to the graveyard, to see all neat and ready where the open grave waited under the precinct wall, covered decorously with planks. The body in its wooden coffin rested on a bier before the parish altar, decently draped. After the Mass it would be carried in procession from the north door, along the Foregate, and in at the great double gate just round the corner from the horse-fair ground, where the laity had access, instead of through the monastic court. A certain separateness must be preserved, for the sake of the quietude necessary to the Rule.

There was a subdued bustle about the great court well before the hour for Mass, brothers hurrying to get their work ready for the rest of the day, or finish small things left undone the previous day. And the people of the Foregate began to gather outside the great west door of the church, or hover about the gatehouse waiting for friends before entering. They came with faces closed and shuttered, dutifully grave and ceremonious, but with quick and careful eyes watching from ambush, uncertain still whether they were really out of the shadow of that resented presence. Perhaps after today they would draw breath and come out of hiding, no longer wary of speaking openly to their neighbours. Perhaps! But what if Hugh should spring his trap in vain?

Cadfael was uneasy about the entire enterprise, but even more dismayed at the thought of this uncertainty continuing for ever, until distrust and fear died at last only from attrition and forgetfulness. Better to have it out into the light, deal with it, and be done. Then at least all but one could be at peace. No – he, too! He most of all!

The notabilities of the Foregate had begun to appear, Erwald the reeve, sombre-faced and aware of his dignity, as befitted and almost justified his use of the title of provost. The smith from his forge, Rhys ab Owain the Welsh farrier – several of the craftsmen of the Foregate were Welsh – Erwald's shepherd kinsman, and Jordan Achard the baker, big and burly and well fleshed, wooden-faced like the rest but nevertheless with a sort of glossy content about him, having survived to bury his detractor. And the little people, too. Aelgar who had worked for the priest and been affronted by the doubt whether he was villein or free, Eadwin whose boundary stone had been shifted by Ailnoth's too close ploughing, Centwin whose child had been buried in unblessed ground and abandoned as lost, the fathers of boys who had learned the hard way to stay out of range of the ebony staff, and shivered in their shoes at having to attend Ailnoth's lessons. The boys themselves gathered at a little distance from their elders, whispering, shuffling, shifting to get a view within but never entering, and sometimes their wary faces showed a sudden fleeting grin here and there, and sometimes their whispering turned briefly to sniggering, half from bravado and half from involuntary awe. The Foregate dogs, sensing the general excitement and unease, ran about between the crowding watchers, snapped edgily at the hooves of passing horses, and loosed volleys of high-pitched barking at every sudden noise.

The women, for the most part, had been left at home. No doubt Jordan's wife was looking after his bakery, raking out the ashes from the early morning firing, and making ready for the second batch, the loaves already shaped and waiting. Just as well for her to be at a safe distance from what was to come, though surely Hugh would not involve the poor soul, when she had only admitted her husband's sleeping abroad in order to save him from this worse accusation. Well, that must be left to Hugh, and Hugh was usually adroit about his manipulations of people and events. But some of the women were here, the elders, the matrons, the widows of solid craftsmen, those who upheld the church even when others became backsliders. The stalwarts at all the least timely services, attending doggedly even at the monastic Vespers as well as the parish Mass, were mostly these sturdy she-elders in their decent black, like lay members of the community itself. They would not miss the ceremonies of this day.

Cadfael was watching the arrivals with a half-attentive gaze and his mind elsewhere, when he saw Diota Hammet come in at the gate, with Sanan's hand solicitous at her elbow. It came both as an anxious reminder and a pleasant refreshment to his eyes, two comely women thus linked in a carefully groomed and perhaps brittle dignity, very calm and stiff with resolution. Autumn and spring came gallantly supporting each other. Ninian in his banishment and solitude would require a full account, and never have an easy moment until he got it. Two hours more and the thing would be done, one way or the other.

They had come in through the gate to the court, and were looking about them, clearly seeking someone. It was Sanan who saw him first, and brightened as she turned to speak quickly into Diota's ear. The widow turned to look, and at once started towards him. He went to meet them, since it seemed he must be the one they were seeking.

'I'm glad to have found you thus before the service,' said

the widow. 'The ointment you gave me – there's the half of it left, and you see I don't need it any more. It would be a shame to waste it, you must have a deal of call for it in this wintry weather.' She had it put away safely in the little bag slung from her girdle, and had to fumble under her cloak to get it out. A small, rough pottery jar, with a wooden lid stoppered tightly into the neck to seal it. She held it out to him on her open palm, and offered him with it a pale but steady smile. 'All my grazes are gone, this can still serve someone else. Take it, with my thanks.'

The last of her grazes, faded now almost to invisibility, hair-fine threads of white, showed elusively round the jar in her palm. The mark on her temple was merely a hyacinth oval, the bruise all but gone.

'You could have kept it against future need, with all my goodwill,' said Cadfael, accepting the offering.

'Well, should I ever have need again, I hope I shall still be here, and able to send to you,' said Diota.

She made him a small, dignified reverence, and turned back towards the church. Over her shoulder Cadfael caught Sanan's confiding blue gaze, harebell-soft and sky-bright, almost as intimate as a signal between conspirators. Then she, too, turned, taking the older woman's arm, and the two of them walked away from him, across the court to the gate, and in at the west door of the church.

Ninian awoke when it was full daylight, thick-headed and slow to collect his wits from having lain half the night wakeful, and then fallen into too profound a slumber. He rose, and swung himself down from the loft without using the ladder, and went out into the fresh, chill, moist morning to shake off the lingering cobwebs. The stalls below were empty. Sanan's man Sweyn had been here already from his own cottage nearer the town, and turned out the two horses into the fenced paddock. They needed a little space for exercise, after the harder frosts when they had been kept indoors, and they were making good use of their freedom, glad of the air and the light. Young and high-spirited and short of work, they would not easily let themselves be caught and bridled, but it was unlikely they would be needed this day.

The cattle byre was still peopled, they would not be let out to the grazing along the riverside until Sweyn was near to keep an eye on them. The byre and stable stood in a large clearing between slopes of woodland, with an open side only to the river, pleasantly private, and under the western stand of trees a little stream ran down to the Severn. Ninian made for it sleepily, stripped off coat and shirt, shivering a little, and plunged head and arms into the water, flinching and drawing in hissing breath at the instant coldness, but taking pleasure in feeling his wits start into warm wakefulness. Shaking off drops from his face and wringing his hands through his thick thatch of curls, he ran a couple of circuits of the open grass at full gallop, caught up his discarded clothes and ran back with them into the shelter of the stable, to scrub himself vigorously with a clean sack until he glowed, and dress himself to face the day. Which might be long and lonely and full of anxieties, but at this moment felt bracing and hopeful.

He had combed his hair into such order as his fingers could command, and was sitting on a bale of straw eating a hunk of bread and an apple from the store Sanan had provided, when he heard the herdsman come along the rough path towards the door. Or was this some other man, and not Sweyn at all? Ninian stiffened to listen, with his cheek bulging with apple, and his jaws motionless. No whistling, and Sweyn always whistled, and these feet came in unusual haste, clearly audible in the rough grass and small stones. Ninian was up in still greater haste, and swung himself up into the loft and hung silent over the hatch, ready for whoever should come.

'Young master . . .' called a voice in the open doorway, without any suggestion of caution. Sweyn, after all, but a Sweyn who had been hurrying, was a little out of breath, and had no thought to spare for whistling this morning. 'Lad, where are you? Come down!'

Ninian let out his breath in a great gust, and slid back through the hatch to hang at arm's length and drop beside the herdsman. 'God's love, Sweyn, you had me reaching for a knife then! I never thought it was you. I thought I had you by heart, by this time, but you came like a stranger. What is it?' He flung an arm about his friend and ally boisterously in his relief, and as quickly held him off to look him up and down from head to foot. 'Lord, lord, in your best, too! In whose honour?'

Sweyn was a thickset, grizzled man of middle age, with a ragged brown beard and a twinkling glance. Whatever warm clothing he put on against the winter he must have put on underneath, for he had but the one stout pair of cloth hose, and Ninian had never yet seen him in any coat but the much-mended drab brown, but evidently he possessed another, for this morning he had on a green coat, unpatched, and a dark brown capuchon protecting head and shoulders.

'I've been into Shrewsbury,' he said shortly, 'fetching a pair of shoes my wife left to be clouted at Provost Corviser's. I was here at first light and let out the horses, they've been penned long enough, and then I went back to fettle myself for the town, and I've had no time to put on my working gear again. There's word going round the town, master, that the sheriff means to attend the Foregate priest's funeral, and fetch a murderer away with him. I thought I'd best bring you word as fast as I could. For it may be true.'

Ninian stood gaping at him aghast for a moment in stricken silence. 'No! He's going to take her? Is that the word? Oh, God, not Diota! And she there to be seized, all unsuspecting. And I not there!' He clutched earnestly at Sweyn's arm. 'Is this certain?'

'It's the common talk about the town. Folks are all agog, there'll be a stream of them making haste over the bridge to see it done. They don't say who – leastways, they guess at it, two or three ways, but they all agree it's coming, be the poor wretch who he may.'

Ninian flung away the apple he had still been holding, and beat his fists together in frantic thought. 'I must go! The parish Mass won't be until ten, there's still time. . . .'

'You can't go. The young mistress said—'

'I know what she said, but this is my business now. I must and will get Diota out of it. Who else can it be the sheriff means to accuse? But he shan't have her! I won't suffer it!'

'You'll be known! It may not be your woman he has in mind, how then? He may have the rights of it, and know well what he's doing. And you'll have thrown yourself away for nothing,' urged the herdsman reasonably.

'No, I needn't be known. One in a crowd – and only the people of the abbey and a few in the Foregate know me well by sight. In any case,' said Ninian grimly, 'let anyone lay a hand on her and I *will* be known, and with a vengeance, too. But I can be lost among a crowd, why not? Lend me that coat and capuchon, Sweyn, who's to know me under a hood? And they've never seen me but in this gear, yours is far too fine for the Benet they've seen about the place. . . .'

'Take the horse,' said Sweyn, stripping off his capuchon without protest, and hoisting the loose cotte over his head.

Ninian did cast one glance out into the field where the two horses kicked up their heels, happy to be at large. 'No, no time! I can do it as fast afoot. And I'd be more noticeable, mounted. How many horsemen will there be about Ailnoth's funeral?' He thrust his way into the over-ample garment already warmed for him, and emerged ruffled and flushed. 'I daren't show a sword. But the dagger I can hide about me.' He was up into the loft to fetch it, and fasten it safely out of sight under his coat, secure in the belt of his hose.

At the doorway, poised to run, he was stricken with another qualm, and turned to clutch again at the herdsman's arm. 'Sweyn, if I'm taken – Sanan will see you shan't be the loser. Your good clothes – I've no right . . .'

'Ah, go on with you!' said Sweyn, half-affronted, and gave him a shove out into the field and towards the trees. 'I can go in sacking if needs must. You bring yourself back safe, or the

168

young mistress will have my head for it. And put up your hood, fool boy, before you come near the road!'

Ninian ran, across the meadow and into the slope of trees, heading for the track that would bring him, within a mile or so, to the Meole Brook, and across it into the Foregate, close by the bridge into the town.

Word of the fat rumour that was running round Shrewsbury reached Ralph Giffard some time later, none of his household having been abroad in the town before nine o'clock, when a maidservant went out to fetch a pitcher of milk, and was a long time about it by reason of the juicy gossip she learned on her errand. Even when she returned to the house the news took some time to be carried from the kitchen to the clerk, who had come to see what all the chatter was about, and thence to Giffard himself, who was at that moment reflecting whether it was not time to leave the town house to the caretaker and make for his chief manor in the north-east. It was pleasant to prolong the comfortable stay here, and he had taken pleasure in falling in with his young son's wish to practise the skills of managing a manor for himself, unsupervised. The boy was sixteen, two years younger than his step-sister, and somewhat jealous of her show of maturity and responsibility in running the distaff side of the household. He was already affianced, a good match with a neighbour's daughter, and naturally he was eager to try his wings. And no doubt he would be doing well enough, and proud of his prowess, but still a father would be only prudent to keep an eye on affairs. There was no bad blood between boy and girl, but for all that, young Ralph would not be sorry to have Sanan safely married and out of the house. If only her marriage did not threaten to cost so much!

'My lord,' said the old clerk, coming in upon his ponderings towards mid morning, 'I think you are rid of your incubus this day, or soon will be. It seems it's all round the town, being bandied across every counter and every doorstep, that Beringar has his murderer known and proved, and means to take him at the priest's burial. And who can it be but that youngster of FitzAlan's? He may have made his escape once, but it seems they've run him to earth this time.'

He brought it as good news, and as such Giffard received it. Once the troublesome fellow was safely in hold, and his own part in the matter as clearly decorous and loyal, he could be at ease. While the rogue ran loose, there might still be unpleasant echoes for any man who had had to do with him.

'So I did well to uncover him,' he said, breathing deeply. 'I might still have been suspect else, when they lay hands on him. Well, well! So the thing's as good as over, and no harm done.'

The thought was very satisfying, even though he would have been just as pleased if it could have been achieved without the act of betrayal with which a lingering scruple in his own mind still reproached him. But now, if it was to be proven that the young fellow really had murdered the priest, then there was no longer need to feel any qualms on his behalf, for he had his deserts.

It was some last superstition that something might yet go wrong, added to a contradictory desire to see the successful consummation in person, that made him think again, and make up his mind, somewhat belatedly, to be in at the death. To make sure, and to wring the fullest savour out of his own preservation.

'After the parish Mass, this was to be? They'll be well into the abbot's sermon by now. I think I'll ride down and see the end of it.' And he was out of his chair and shouting across the yard for the groom to saddle his horse.

Abbot Radulfus had been speaking for some time, slowly, with the high, withdrawn voice of intense thought, every word measured. In the choir it was always dim, a parable of the life of man, a small, lighted space arched over by a vast shadowy darkness, for even in darkness there are degrees of shadow. The crowded nave was lighter, and with so many people in attendance not even notably cold. When choir

170

monks and secular congregation met for worship together, the separation between them seemed accentuated rather than softened. We here, you out there, thought Brother Cadfael, and yet we are all like flesh, and our souls subject to the same final judgement.

'The company of the saints,' said Abbot Radulfus, his head raised so that he looked rather into the vault than at those he addressed, 'is not to be determined by any measure within our understanding. It cannot be made up of those without sin, for who that ever wore flesh, except one, can make so high a claim? Surely there is room within it for those who have set before themselves lofty aims, and done their best to reach them, and so, we believe, did our brother and shepherd here dead. Yes, even though they fail of attaining their aims, more, even though those aims may have been too narrow, the mind that conceived them being blinded by prejudice and pride, and channelled too greedily towards a personal excellence. For even the pursuit of perfection may be sin, if it infringes the rights and needs of another soul. Better to fail a little, by turning aside to lift up another, than to pass by him in haste to reach our own reward, and leave him to solitude and despair. Better to labour in lameness, in fallibility, but holding up others who falter, than to stride forward alone.

'Again, it is not enough to abstain from evil, there must also be an outgoing goodness. The company of the blessed may extend justifiably to embrace even men who have been great sinners, yet also great lovers of their fellow men, such as have never turned away their eyes from other men's needs, but have done them such good as they might, and as little harm as they must. For in that they saw a neighbour's need, they saw God's need, as he himself has shown us, and inasmuch as they saw a neighbour's face more clearly than their own, so also they saw God's face.

'Further, I show you certainly that all such as are born into this world and die untainted by personal sin partake of the martyred purity of the Holy Innocents, and die for Our Lord, who also will embrace them and quicken them living, where they shall no more partake of death. And if they died without name here, yet their name is written in his book, and no other need know it, until the day come.

'But we, all we who share the burden of sin, it behoves us not to question or fret concerning the measure dealt out to us, or try to calculate our own merit and deserving, for we have not the tools by which to measure values concerning the soul. That is God's business. Rather it behoves us to live every day as though it were our last, to the full of such truth and kindness as is within us, and to lie down every night as though the next day were to be our first, and a new and pure beginning. The day will come when all will be made plain. Then shall we know, as now we trust. And in that trust we commit our pastor here to the care of the shepherd of shepherds, in the sure hope of the resurrection.'

He uttered the blessing with his face lowered at last to those who listened. Probably he wondered how many had understood, and how many, indeed, had need of understanding.

It was over here, people stirred stealthily in the nave, sliding towards the north door to be first out and secure a good place ahead of the procession. In the choir the three ministering priests, abbot, prior and sub-prior, descended to the bier, and the brothers formed silent file, two by two, after them. The party of bearers took up the burden, and made towards the open north doorway into the Foregate. How is it, thought Cadfael, watching, and glad of a distraction, however sinful at such a moment, how is it that there is always one out of step, or just a little too short in height and stride to match the others? Is it so that we should not fall into the error of taking even death too seriously?

It was no great surprise to find the Foregate crowded when the procession issued from the north porch and turned to the right along the precinct wall, but at first glance it did come as a surprise to find half the townspeople among the starers, as well as the men of the parish. Then Cadfael understood the reason. Hugh had had discreet whispers of his plans leaked within the town walls, too late for them to be carried out here to the folk most concerned, and give warning, but in time to bring the worthies of Shrewsbury – or perhaps even more surely the unworthies, who had time to waste on curiosity – hurrying here to be witnesses of the ending.

Cadfael was still wondering what that ending was to be. Hugh's device might provoke some man's conscience and make him speak out, to deliver a neighbour mistakenly accused, but equally it might come as an immense relief to the guilty, and be accepted as a gift – certainly not from heaven, rather from the other place! At every step along the Foregate he fretted at the tangle of details churning in his mind, and found no coherence among them. Not until the little jar of ointment he had thrust into the breast of his habit nodded against his middle as his foot slid in a muddy rut. The touch was like an impatient nudge at his mind. He saw it again, resting in the palm of a shapely but work-worn hand, as Diota held it out to him. A hand seamed with the lines proper to the human palm, graven deep with lifelong use, but also bearing thread-like white lines that crossed these, fanning from wrist to fingers, barely visible now, soon to vanish altogether.

An icy night, certainly, he had trodden cautiously through it himself, he knew. And a woman slipping as she turned to step back on to the frozen doorstone of a house, and falling forward, naturally puts out her hands to save herself, and her hands take the rough force of the fall, even though they may not quite save her head. Except that Diota had not fallen. Her head injury was sustained in quite a different way. She had fallen on her knees that night, yes, but of desperate intent, with hands clutching not at frozen ground, but at the skirts of Ailnoth's cassock and cloak. So how did she get those scored grazes in both palms?

In innocence she had told him but half a story, believing she told him all. And here was he helpless now, he must hold his place in this funeral procession, and she must hold hers, and he could not get to her, to probe the corners of memory

173

which had eluded her then. Not until this solemn rite was over and done would he be able to speak again with Diota. No, but there were other witnesses, mute by their nature but possibly eloquent in what they might be able to demonstrate. He walked on perforce, keeping pace with Brother Henry along the Foregate and round the corner by the horse-fair ground, unable to break the decorum of burial. Not yet! But perhaps within? For there would be no procession through the street afterwards, not for the brethren. They would be already within their chosen enclave, to disperse severally to their ablutions and their dinner in the refectory. Once within, why should he be missed if he slipped quietly away?

The broad double doors in the precinct wall stood wide open to let the mourning column into the wide prospect of the cemetery garth, giving place on the left to kitchen gardens, and beyond, the long roof of the abbot's lodging, and the small enclosed flower garden round it. The brothers were buried close under the east end of the church, the vicars of the parish a little removed from them, but in the same area. The number of graves as yet was not large, the foundation being no more than fifty-eight years old, and though the parish was older, it had then been served by the small wooden church Earl Roger had replaced in stone and given to the newly founded abbey. There were trees here, and grass, and meadow flowers in the summer, a pleasant enough place. Only the dark, raw hole close to the wall marred the green enclosure. Cynric had placed trestles to receive the coffin before it was lowered into the grave, and he was stooped over the planks he had just removed, stacking them tidily against the wall.

Half the Foregate and a good number of the inhabitants of the town came thronging through the open doors after the brothers, crowding close to see all there was to be seen. Cadfael drew back from his place in the ranks, and contrived to be swallowed up by their inquisitive numbers. No doubt Brother Henry would eventually miss him from his side, but in the circumstances he would say no word. By the time Prior Robert had got out the first sonorous phrases of the committal, Cadfael was round the corner of the chapter house and scurrying across the great court towards the wicket by the infirmary, that led through to the mill.

Hugh had brought down with him from the castle two sergeants and two of the young men of the garrison, all mounted, though they had left their horses tethered at the abbey gatehouse, and allowed the funeral procession to make its way along the Foregate to the cemetery before they showed themselves. While all eyes were on the prior and the coffin Hugh posted two men outside the open doors, to make a show of preventing any departures, while he and the sergeants went within, and made their way unobtrusively forward through the press. The very discretion with which they advanced, and the respectful silence they preserved when they had drawn close to the bier, which should have kept them inconspicuous, perversely drew every eye, so that by the time they were where Hugh had designed they should be, himself almost facing the prior across the coffin, the sergeants a pace or two behind Jordan Achard, one on either side, many a furtive glance had turned on them, and there was a wary shifting and staring and stealthy shuffling of feet on all sides. But Hugh held his hand until all was over.

Cynric and his helpers hoisted the coffin, and fitted the slings to lower it into the grave. Earth fell dully. The last prayer was said. There was the inevitable stillness and hush, before everyone would sigh and stir, and very slowly begin to move away. The sigh came like a sudden gust of wind, it fell from so many throats. The stir followed like the rustle of leaves in the gust. And Hugh said loudly and clearly, in a voice calculated to arrest any movement on the instant:

'My lord abbot, Father Prior . . . I must ask your pardon for having placed a guard at your gate – outside your walls, but even so I beg your indulgence. No one must leave here until I've made known my purpose. Hold me excused that I must come at such a time, but there's no help for it. I am here in the name of the King's law, and in pursuit of a murderer. I am here to take into charge a felon suspected of the slaying of Father Ailnoth.'

Chapter Twelve

There was not very much to be found, but there was enough. Cadfael stood on the rim of the high bank where Ailnoth's body had bobbed and nestled, held fast there by the slight side impulse from the tail-race of the mill. The stump of the felled willow, no more than hip-high, bristled with its whips of blanched green hair. Some broken shoots among them, at the rim of the barren, dead surface, dried and cracked with time and jagged from the axe. And a finger length of black thread fluttering, one end securely held in the frayed ridge of dead wood. A finger length of unravelled woollen braid, just enough to complete the binding of a black skull-cap. Frost and thaw had come and gone, whitened and moistened and changed and obliterated whatever else had once been there to be found, a smear of blood, perhaps, some minute fragments of torn skin. Nothing left but a fluttering black roving, clawed loose when the cap flew wide and went with the current into the reeds.

Cadfael went back in haste with the infinitesimal scrap of wool in his hand. Halfway across the great court he heard the clamour of voices howling protest, excitement and confusion, and slackened his pace, for clearly there was no more need for haste. The trap was sprung, and must hold whatever it caught. Too late to prevent, at least he could undo whatever harm came of it, and if none came, so much the better. What he had to say and to show would keep.

Ninian reached the open track and the bridge over the Meole Brook in a glow from running most of the way, and remembered to slow to a walk before he reached the highway, close to the end of the bridge into Shrewsbury, and to haul up the hood of Sweyn's capuchon to shadow his face. At the turning into the Foregate he first checked in mild alarm, and then realised his luck and took heart, for so many people were still hurrying out of the town towards the abbey that it was very simple to mingle with them and be lost. He went with the stream, ears pricked for every word uttered around him, and heard his own name bandied back and forth with anticipatory relish. So that was the arrest some of these were expecting, though it could hardly be what Hugh Beringar had in mind, since he had lost the scent some days ago, and had no reason to suppose that he would recover it today. But others spoke of the woman, the priest's servant, not even knowing a name by which to call her. Others again were speculating wildly between two or three names unknown to Ninian, but who had evidently suffered under Ailnoth's unbending severities.

It seemed he had come only in time to join the stragglers in the traffic from the town, those who had been late in hearing the gossip, for the Foregate from the gatehouse of the abbey on was already crowded. Just as Ninian reached the gatehouse the clergy were emerging from the north door, and after them the coffin, and all the brothers in solemn procession. This was the one danger he must avoid, at least until he knew whether he had to face the worst, and deliver himself up of his own will. These were the men, any one of whom might know him on sight if he caught a clear glimpse of his face, indeed might be able to place him even by his build and gait. He withdrew hastily, weaving between the curious watchers to the far side of the street, and slipped into the mouth of the narrow alley until the monks had all passed by. After them came those of the parish worthies whose dignity had forbidden them to scurry first out of the church and secure a favourable place in the cemetery garth. And after them streamed the watchers in the Foregate, intent and avid as children and dogs after a travelling tumbler, though not so candidly loud in their anticipation of wonders.

To be the last and alone would be as bad as thrusting himself to the fore. Ninian slid out of concealment in time to join the rear guard, and hung just within the fringes as the cortège made its way along the Foregate to the corner by the horse-fair, and rounded it to the cemetery doors, which stood wide open.

There were a few besides himself, it seemed, who wanted to see everything there was to be seen, without making themselves conspicuous, and likewise preferred to hang upon the fringes of the crowd outside the gates, peering within. And that might be because two men of the castle garrison stood one on either side the entrance, very casually, not interfering with those who went in, but nevertheless to be eyed with caution.

Ninian halted in the wide opening, neither in nor out, and peered forward, craning to see between the massed heads, and reach the group gathered about the grave. Both abbot and prior were more than commonly tall, he could see them clearly above the rest, and hear the prayers of the committal ring aloud in Prior Robert's consciously mellifluous tones, to reach every ear. The prior had a genuinely splendid voice, and loved to exercise it in all the highly dramatic possibilities of the liturgy.

Edging a step or two to one side, Ninian caught a glimpse of Diota's face, a pale oval under her black hood. She stood close beside the bier, her due as the only member of the priest's household. The curve of a shoulder pressed close to hers, the arm linked in her arm, could only belong to Sanan, though no matter how he craned to one side and the other, he could not get a view of the beloved face, taller heads moved always between.

There was a ripple of movement as the priests advanced to the grave-side, the crowd swinging that way with them. The coffin was being lowered, the last dismissal spoken. Under the high precinct wall the first clods of earth fell on Father Ailnoth's coffin. It was almost over, and nothing had broken the decorum of the occasion. The first shuffle and rustle and stir passed through the assembly, acknowledging an ending. Ninian's heart settled in him, cautiously hoping, and as suddenly seemed to heave over in his breast as another voice, raised to carry clearly, spoke up from the grave-side:

'My lord abbot, Father Prior . . . I must ask your pardon for having placed a guard at your gate. . . .'

For the beating of the blood in his ears Ninian missed what came next, but he knew the voice must belong to the sheriff, for who else bore such authority even here, within the enclave? And the end he heard all too clearly: 'I am here to take into charge a felon suspected of the slaying of Father Ailnoth.'

So the worst had fallen on them, after all, just as rumour had foretold. There was a sudden stunned silence, and then a great buzz of confusion and excitement that shook the crowd like a gale of wind. The next words were lost, though Ninian held his breath and strained to hear. Some of those standing with him outside the gate had pressed forward, to miss nothing of this sensation, and no one had any ears for the clatter of hooves coming briskly round the corner by the horse-fair, and heading towards them at a trot. Within the walls there came a sudden wild outcry, a babel of voices exclaiming and protesting, bombarding those before them with questions, passing back probably inaccurate answers to those behind. Ninian braced himself to plunge in and shoulder his way through to where his womenfolk stood embattled and defenceless. For it was over, his liberty was forfeit, if not his life. He drew breath deep, and laid his hand on the shoulder of the nearest body that barred his way, for the curious had abandoned caution and filled up the open gateway.

The bellow of dismay and indignation that suddenly rose from under the precinct wall stopped him in his tracks and hurled him back almost physically from the doorway. A man's voice, howling protests, calling heaven to witness his innocence. Not Diota! Not Diota, but a man!

'My lord, I swear to you I know nothing of it. . . . I never saw hide or hair of him that day or that night. I was fast at home, my wife will tell you so! I never harmed any man, much less a priest. . . . Someone has lied about me, lied! My lord abbot, as God sees me . . .'

The name was borne back to Ninian's ears rank by rank through the crowd. 'Jordan Achard . . . it was Jordan Achard. . . . They're seizing Jordan Achard. . . .'

Ninian stood trembling, weak with reaction, and so neglectful of his own situation that he had let the hood of Sweyn's capuchon slip back from his head and lie in folds on his shoulders. Behind him the hooves had halted, shifting lightly in the thin mud of the thaw.

'Hey, you, fellow!'

The butt of a whip jabbed him sharply in the back, and he swung about, startled, to look up directly into the face of a rider who leaned down to him from the saddle of a fine roan horse. A big, ruddy, sinewy man in his fifties, perhaps, very spruce in his own gear and the accoutrements of his mount, and with the nobleman's authority in his voice and face. A handsome face, bearded and strong-featured, now just beginning to run to flesh and lose its taut, clear lines, but still memorable. The brief moment they spent staring closely at each other was terminated by a second impatient but good-natured prod of the whip's butt against Ninian's shoulder, and the brisk order:

'Yes, you, lad! Hold my horse while I'm within, and you shan't be the loser. What's afoot in there, do you know? Someone's making a fine noise about it.'

In the exuberance of relief from his terror for Diota, Ninian rebounded into impudent glee, knuckled his forehead obsequiously, and reached willingly for the bridle, once again the penniless peasant groom Benet to the life. 'I don't rightly know, master,' he said, 'but there's some in there saying a man's been taken up for killing the priest. . . .' He smoothed a hand over the horse's silken forehead and between the pricked ears, and the roan tossed his head, turned a soft, inquisitive muzzle to breathe warmth at him, and accepted the caress graciously. 'A lovely beast, my lord! I'll mind him well.'

'So the murderer's taken, is he? Rumour told truth for once.' The rider was down in a moment, and off through the quivering crowd like a sickle cutting grass, a brusque, hard shoulder forward and a masterful tongue ready to demand passage. Ninian was left with his cheek against a glossy shoulder, and a tangle of feelings boiling within him, laughter and gratitude, and the joyful anticipation of a journey now free from all regrets and reservations, but also a small, bitter jet of sadness that one man was dead untimely, and another now accused of his murder. It took him some little time to remember to pull the hood over his head again, and well forward to shadow his face, but luckily all attention was fixed avidly upon the hubbub within the cemetery garth, and no one was paying any heed to a hind holding his master's horse in the street. The horse was excellent cover, but it did prevent him from advancing again into the wide-open doorway, and even by straining his ears he could make little sense out of the babel from within. The clamour of terrified protest went on for some time, that was plain enough, and the shrill commentary from the bystanders made a criss-cross of conflicting sounds around it. If there were saner voices speaking, Hugh Beringar's or the abbot's, they were drowned in the general chaos.

Ninian leaned his forehead against the warm hide that quivered gently under his touch, and offered devout thanks for so timely a deliverance.

In the heart of the tumult Abbot Radulfus raised a voice that seldom found it necessary to thunder, and thundered to instant effect.

'Silence! You bring shame on yourselves and desecrate this holy place. Silence, I say!'

And there was silence, sudden and profound, though it might as easily break out in fresh chaos if the rein was not tightened.

182

'So, and keep silence, all you who have nothing here to plead or deny. Let those speak and be heard who have. Now, my lord sheriff, you accuse this man Jordan Achard of murder. On what evidence?'

'On the evidence,' said Hugh, 'of a witness who has said and will say again that he lies in saying he spent that night at home. Why, if he has nothing to hide, should he find it necessary to lie? On the evidence also of a witness who saw him creeping out from the mill path and making for his home at earliest light on Christmas morning. It is enough to hold him upon suspicion,' said Hugh crisply, and motioned to the two sergeants, who grasped the terrified Jordan almost tenderly by the arms. 'That he had a grievance against Father Ailnoth is known to everyone.'

'My lord abbot,' babbled Jordan, quaking, 'on my soul I swear I never touched the priest. I never saw him, I was not there . . . it's false . . . they lie about me. . . .'

'It seems there are those,' said Radulfus, 'who will equally swear that you were there.'

'It was I who told that I'd seen him,' spoke up the reeve's shepherd cousin, worried and shaken by the result he had achieved. 'I could say no other, for I did see him, and it was barely light, and all I've told is truth. But I never intended mischief, and I never thought any harm but that he was at his games, for I knew what's said of him. . . .'

'And what is said of you, Jordan?' asked Hugh mildly.

Jordan swallowed and writhed, agonised between shame at owning where he had spent his night, and terror of holding out and risking worse. Sweating and wriggling, he blurted: 'No evil, I'm a man well respected. . . . If I was there, it was for no wrong purpose. I . . . I had business there early, charitable business there early – with the old Widow Warren who lives along there. . . . .'

'Or late, with her slut of a maidservant,' called a voice from the safe anonymity of the crowd, and a great ripple of laughter went round, hastily suppressed under the abbot's flashing glare.

'Was that the truth of it? And by chance under Father Ailnoth's eye?' demanded Hugh. 'He would look very gravely upon such depravity, from all accounts. Did he catch you sneaking into the house, Jordan? I hear he was apt to reprove sin on the spot, and harshly. Is that how you came to kill him and leave him in the pool?'

'I never did!' howled Jordan. 'I swear I never had ado with him. If I did fall into sin with the girl, that was all I did. I never went past the house. Ask her, she'll tell you! I was there all night long. . . .'

And all this time Cynric had gone on patiently and steadily filling in the grave, without haste, without apparently paying any great attention to all the tumult at his back. During this last exchange he had straightened up creakily, and stretched until his joints cracked. Now he turned to thrust his way into the centre of the circle, the iron-shod spade still dangling in his hand.

So strange an intrusion from so solitary and withdrawn a man silenced all voices and drew all eyes.

'Let him be, my lord,' said Cynric. 'Jordan had nought to do with the man's death.' He turned his greying head and long, sombre, deep-eyed face from Hugh to the abbot, and back again. 'There's none but I,' he said simply, 'knows how Ailnoth came by his end.'

Then there was utter silence, beyond what the abbot's authority had been able to invoke, a silence deep enough to drown in, as Ailnoth had drowned. The verger stood tall and dignified in his rusty black, waiting to be questioned further, without fear or regret, seeing nothing strange in what he had said, and no reason why he should have said more or said it earlier, but willing to bear with those who demanded explanations.

'You know?' said the abbot, after long and astonished contemplation of the man before him. 'And you have not spoken before?'

'I saw no need. There was no other soul put in peril, not till now. The thing was done, best leave well alone.'

'Are you saying,' demanded Radulfus doubtfully, 'that you were there, that you witnessed it? . . . Was it *you* . . .?'

'No,' said Cynric with a slow shake of his long, grizzled head. 'I did not touch him.' His voice was patient and gentle, as it would have been to questioning children. 'I was there, I witnessed it. But I did not touch him.'

'Then tell us now,' said Hugh quietly. 'Who killed him?'

'No one killed him,' said Cynric. 'Those who do violence die by the same. It's only just.'

'Tell us,' said Hugh again as softly. 'Tell us how this befell. Let us all know, and be at peace again. You are saying his death was an accident?'

'No accident,' said Cynric, and his eyes burned in their deep sockets. 'A judgement.'

He moistened his lips, and lifted his head to stare into the wall of the Lady Chapel, above their heads, as if he, who was illiterate, could read there the words he had to say, he who was a man of few words by nature.

'I went out that night to the pool. I have often walked there by night, when there has been no moon, and none awake to see. Between the willow trees there, beyond the mill, where she went into the water . . . Eluned, Nest's girl . . . because Ailnoth refused her confession and the uses of the church, denounced her before all the parish and shut the door in her face. He could as well have stabbed her to the heart, it would have been kinder. All that brightness and beauty taken from us. . . . I knew her well, she came so often for comfort while Father Adam lived, and he never failed her. And when she was not fretting over her sins she was like a bird, like a flower, a joy to see. There are not so many things of beauty in the world that a man should destroy one of them, and make no amends. And when she fell into remorse she was like a child . . . she *was* a child, it was a child he cast out. . . .'

He fell silent for a moment, as though the words had become hard to read by reason of the blindness of grief, and furrowed his high forehead to decipher them the better, but no one ventured to speak.

'There I was standing, where Eluned went into the pool, when he came along the path. I did not know who it was, he did not come as far as where I stood – but someone, a man stamping and muttering, there by the mill. A man in a rage, or so it sounded. Then a woman came stumbling after him, I heard her cry out to him, she went on her knees to him, weeping, and he was trying to shake her off, and she would not let go of him. He struck her – I heard the blow. She made no more than a moan, but then I did go towards them, thinking there could be murder done, and therefore I saw – dimly, but I had my night eyes, and I did see – how he swung his stick at her again, and she clung with both hands to the head of it to save herself, and how he tugged at it with all his strength and tore it out of her hands. . . . The woman ran from him, I heard her stumbling away along the path, but I doubt she ever heard what I heard, or knows what I know. I heard him reel backwards and crash into the stump of the willow. I heard the withies lash and break. I heard the splash – it was not a great sound – as he went into the water.'

There was another silence, long and deep, while he thought, and laboured to remember with precision, since that was required of him. Brother Cadfael, coming up quietly behind the ranks of the awestruck brothers, had heard only the latter part of Cynric's story, but he had the poor, draggled proof of it in his hand as he listened. Hugh's trap had caught nothing, rather it had set everyone free. He looked across the mute circle to where Diota stood, with Sanan's arm about her. Both women had drawn their hoods close round their faces. One of the hands torn by the sharp edges of the silver band held the folds of Diota's cloak together.

'I went towards the place,' said Cynric, 'and looked into the water. It was only then I knew him certainly for Ailnoth. He drifted at my feet, stunned or dazed. . . . I knew his face. His eyes were open. . . . And I turned my back and walked away from him, as he turned his back on her and walked away from her, shutting the door on her tears as he struck at this other woman's tears. . . . If God had willed him to live, he would have lived. Why else should it happen there, in that very place? And who am I, to usurp the privilege of God?'

All this he delivered in the same reasonable voice with which he would have rendered account of the number of candles bought for the parish altar, though the words came slowly and with effort and thought, studying to make all plain now that plainness was needed. But to Abbot Radulfus it had some distant echo of the voice of prophecy. Even if the man had wished to save, could he have saved? Might not the priest have been already past saving? And there in the dark, alone, with no time to summon help, since everyone was preparing for the night office, and with that undercut bank to contend with, and the dead weight of a big man to handle – could any man, singly, have saved? Better to suppose that the thing had been impossible, and accept what to Cynric was the will of God!

'And now, with your leave, my lord abbot,' said Cynric, having waited courteously but vainly for some comment or question, 'if you've no more need of me I'll be getting on with filling in the grave, for I'll need the most of the daylight to make a good job of it.'

'Do so,' said the abbot, and looked at him for a moment, eye to eye, with no shadow of blame, and saw no shadow of doubt. 'Do so, and come to me for your fee when it is done.'

Cynric went as he had come, back to his work, and those who watched him in awe-stricken silence saw no change in his long-legged walk, or in the quiet, steady rhythm with which he plied his spade.

Radulfus looked at Hugh, and then to Jordan Achard, mute and wilting with relief from terror between his guards. For a brief instant the abbot's austere face was shaken by the merest fleeting shadow of a smile. 'My lord sheriff, I think your charge against this man is already answered. What other offences he may have on his conscience,' said the abbot, fixing the demoralised Jordan with a severe eye, 'I recommend him to bring to confession. And to avoid henceforward!

He may well reflect on the dangers into which such a manner of life has led him, and take this day as a warning.'

'For my part, I'm glad to know the truth and find that none of us here has the guilt of murder on his soul,' said Hugh. 'Master Achard, take yourself home and be glad you have a loyal and dutiful wife. Lucky for you there was one here to speak for you, for there was a strong case against you had there been no such witness. Loose him!' he said to his sergeants. 'Let him be about his business. By rights he owes a gift to the parish altar, by way of thanks for a good deliverance.'

Jordan all but sagged to the ground when the two officers took their hands from him, and Will Warden was moved in good humour to lend him a supporting hand again under one arm until he got his legs to stand solid under him. And now at last it was truly over, but that every soul there was so petrified with wonder that it took another benediction by way of dismissal to start them moving.

'Go now, good people,' said the abbot, somewhat brusquely accepting the need. 'Make your prayers for the soul of Father Ailnoth, and bear in mind that our neighbour's failings should but make us mindful rather of our own. Go, and trust to us who have the grant of this parish to bestow, to consider your needs above all in whatever we determine.' And he blessed them departing, with a vigour and brevity that actually set them in motion. Silent as yet, even as they melted like snow and began to move away, but soon they would be voluble enough. Town and Foregate would ring with the many and contradictory accounts of this morning's events, to be transmuted at last into myth, a folk memory of momentous things witnessed, once, long ago.

'And you, brothers,' said Radulfus shortly, turning to his own flock, doves with fluttered feathers now and disrupted cooing, 'go now to your daily duties, and make ready for dinner.'

They broke ranks almost fearfully, and drifted apart as the

rest were doing, apparently aimlessly at first, then making slowly for the places where now they should be. Like sparks from a fire, or dust scattered on a wind, they disseminated, still half-dazed with revelation. The only one who went about his business with purpose and method was Cynric, busy with his spade under the wall.

Brother Jerome, deeply disturbed by proceedings which in no way fitted in with his conception of the rule and routine of the Benedictine order, went about rounding up some of his strayed chicks towards the lavatorium and the frater, and shooing some of the lingering parishioners out of the abbey's confines. In so doing he drew near to the wide-open doors upon the Foregate, and became aware of a young man standing in the street outside, holding the bridle of a horse, and casting an occasional brief glance over those emerging, but from within a close-drawn capuchon, so that his face was not clearly visible. But there was something about him that held Jerome's sharp eyes. Something not quite recognised, since the coat and capuchon were strange, and the face obstinately averted, and yet something reminiscent of a certain young fellow known for a while to the brethren, and later vanished in strange circumstances. If only the fellow would once turn his face fully!

Cadfael, lingering to watch Sanan and Diota depart, saw them instead draw back into the shadow of the chapel wall, and wait there until the greater part of the throng had moved towards the Foregate. The impulse came from Sanan, he saw her restraining hand laid upon the older woman's arm, and wondered why she should delay. Had she seen someone among the crowd whom she was anxious not to encounter? In search of such a person, he scanned the retreating backs, and saw one at least whose presence there would certainly not be too welcome to her. And had she not, like Diota, drawn the hood of her cloak closely round her face, during the time that Cadfael himself had been absent, as if to avoid being noticed and recognised by someone?

Now the two women began to move after the rest, but

with cautious slowness, and Sanan's eyes were intent upon the back of the tall man who had almost reached the open doorway. Thus both Sanan and Cadfael at the same moment also saw Brother Jerome, hovering hesitant for a moment, and then making purposefully for the street. And following the converging courses of these two very dissimilar backs, the one erect and confident, the other meagre and stooped, inevitably lighted upon the horse waiting in the Foregate, and the young man holding his bridle.

Brother Jerome was still not quite sure, though he was bent on making sure, even if it meant leaving the precinct without due reason or permission. It would be counted due reason enough if he succeeded in raising a righteous alarm, and handing over a fugitive enemy of the King to the King's justice. A guard outside the gates, the sheriff had said. He had but to halloo the soldiers on to their quarry, who stood within arm's reach, believing himself safe. If, of course, *if* this really was the youngster once known as Benet?

But if Jerome was not yet certain, Sanan was, and Cadfael was. Who, in these parts, had known that figure and stance and carriage as well as they? And there was Jerome bearing down upon him with plainly malevolent intent, before their eyes, and they had no way of preventing the disaster.

Sanan dropped Diota's arm and started forward. Cadfael, approaching from another angle, bellowed: '*Brother!*' peremptorily after Jerome, in a self-righteous and scandalised voice of which Jerome himself need not have been ashamed, in the hope of diverting his attention, but vainly. Jerome nose-down on the trail of a malefactor was almost as undeflectable as Father Ailnoth himself. It was left to someone else to turn the trick.

Ninian's horseman, long-legged and striding briskly away from a field which left him unthreatened and well satisfied, arrived at the doorway only a pace or two ahead of Jerome, indeed he brushed past him into the Foregate. Not the ending he had expected, but on the whole he was glad of it. As long as he was neither suspect of disloyalty nor threatened with loss of lands of status, he bore no grudge now against the rash young man who had caused him so much anxiety. Let him get away unscathed, provided he never came back here to make trouble for others.

Ninian had glanced round to see his patron approaching, and saw at the same time, very belatedly, the ferret countenance of Brother Jerome, all too clearly making for him with no kindly intent. There was no time to evade, he had no choice but to stand his ground. Blessedly the horseman reached him barely ahead of the hunter, and blessedly he was well content with whatever he had witnessed within, for he clapped his horse-boy on the shoulder as the bridle was surrendered into his hand. Ninian made haste to stoop to the stirrup, and hold it for the rider to mount.

It was enough! Jerome stopped so abruptly in the gateway that Erwald, coming behind, collided with him, and put him aside good-naturedly with one large hand as he passed. And by that time the horseman had dropped a careless word of thanks into Ninian's ear and a silver penny into his hand, and set off back along the Foregate at a leisurely trot, to vanish round the corner by the horse-fair ground, with his supposed groom loping behind him on foot.

A lucky escape, thought Ninian, dropping into a walk as soon as he was round the corner of the high wall and out of sight. And he span delightedly in his hand the silver penny a satisfied and lavish patron had tossed to him as he rode away. God bless the man, whoever he may be, he's saved my life, or at least my hide! A man of consequence, and evidently well known here. Just as well for me his grooms are not equally well known, and all over fifty and bearded, or I should have been a lost man.

A lucky escape, thought Cadfael, heaving a great sigh of relief, and turning back to where Hugh still stood in earnest talk with Abbot Radulfus, under the great east window of the Lady Chapel. Salvation comes from strange places and unexpected friends. And a very apt ending, too!

A lucky escape, thought Sanan, shaking with dismay and fear suddenly transmuted into triumphant laughter. And he has no idea what has just happened! Neither of them has! Oh, to see Ninian's face when I tell him!

A lucky escape, thought Jerome, scurrying thankfully back to his proper duties. I should have made a sorry fool of myself if I had challenged him. A mere chance resemblance in figure and bearing, after all, nothing more. What a blessing for me that his master brushed by in time to acknowledge him as his, and warn me of my error.

For of course, Ralph Giffard, of all people, could scarcely be harbouring in his own service the very man he himself had so properly denounced to the law!

Chapter Thirteen

'There is one question,' said the abbot, 'which not only has not been answered, it has not yet been asked.'

He had waited until the table was cleared, and his guest supplied with the final cup of wine. Radulfus never allowed business of any kind to be discussed during a meal. The pleasures of the table were something he used sparingly, but respected.

'What is that?' asked Hugh.

'Has he told all the truth?'

Hugh looked up sharply across the table. 'Cynric? Who can say of any man that he never lies? But general report of Cynric says that he never speaks at all unless he must, and then to the point. It is why he said nothing until Jordan was accused. Words come very hard to Cynric. I doubt if he ever in his life used as many in one day as we heard from him in a handful of moments this morning. I doubt if he would waste breath on lying, when even necessary truth costs him such labour.'

'He was eloquent enough today,' said Radulfus with a wry smile. 'But I should be glad if we had some sure sign to confirm what he told us. He may very well have done no more than turn and walk away, and leave the issue of life and death to God, or whatever force he regards as the arbiter of justice in such a strange case. Or he may have struck the blow himself. Or he may have seen the thing happen, much as he says, but helped the priest into the water while he was stunned. Granted I do not think Cynric would be very ingenious at making up plausible tales to cover the event, yet we cannot *know*. Nor do I think him at all a man of violence, even where he found much to provoke it, but again we cannot *know*. And even if we have the entire truth from him, what should be done about such a man? How proceed with him?'

'For my part,' said Hugh firmly, 'nothing can or will be done. There is no law he has broken. It may be a sin to allow a death to take place, it is not a crime. I hold fast to my own writ. Sinners are in your province, not mine.' He did not add that there was some accounting due from the man who had brought Ailnoth, a stranger scarcely known, to assume the pastoral care of a bereaved flock that had no voice in the choosing of their new shepherd. But he suspected that the thought was in the abbot's mind, and had been ever since the first complaints were brought to his ears. He was not a man to shut his eyes to his own errors, or shirk his own responsibilities.

'This I can tell you,' said Hugh. 'What he said of the woman who followed Ailnoth and was struck down by him is certainly true. Mistress Hammet claimed then that she had fallen on the icy ground. That was a lie. The priest did that to her, she has owned it since to Brother Cadfael, who treated her injuries. And since I have now brought Cadfael into this, I think you would do well, my lord, to send for him. I have had no chance to speak with him since the events of this morning, and it's in my mind that he may have something further to say in this matter. He was missing from the ranks of the brothers in the cemetery when I came, for I looked for him and couldn't find him. He came later, not from the Foregate but from within the court. He would not have absented himself but for good reason. If he has things to tell me, I cannot afford to neglect them.'

'Neither, it seems, can I,' said Radulfus, and reached for the little bell that lay on his desk. The small silver chime brought in his secretary from the ante-room. 'Brother Vitalis, will you find Brother Cadfael, and ask him to come here to us?'

194

When the door had closed again the abbot sat silent for a while, considering. 'I know now, of course,' he said at last, 'that Father Ailnoth was indeed grossly deceived, and that is some extenuation for him. But the woman – I gather she is no kin to the youth she sheltered, the one we knew as Benet? – she had been an exemplary servant to her master for three years, her only offence was in protecting the young man, an offence which sprang only from affection. There shall be no penalty visited upon her, never by my authority. She shall have quiet living here, since it was I who brought her here. If we get a new priest who has neither mother nor sister to mind his dwelling, then she may serve him as she did Ailnoth, and I hope there may never be reason for her to kneel to him but in the confessional, and none ever for him to strike her. And as for the boy . . .' He looked back with a resigned and tolerant eye, and shook his head a little, smiling. 'I remember we gave him to Cadfael to do the rough work before the winter freeze. I saw him once in the garden, digging the long butt. At least he gave honest value. FitzAlan's squire was not afraid to dig, nor ashamed.' He looked up, head tilted, into Hugh's face. 'You don't, by any chance, know . . .?'

'I have been rather careful not to know,' said Hugh.

'Well . . . I am glad he never fouled his hands with murder. I saw them black enough with soil, from plucking out the weeds too gross to be dug in,' said Radulfus, and smiled distantly, looking out of the window at a pearl-grey, low hanging sky. 'I expect he'll do well enough. Pity of all pities there should be one such young man in arms against another in this land, but at least let the steel be bared only in the open field, not privily in the dark.'

Cadfael laid out on the abbot's desk the remaining relics of Father Ailnoth, the ebony staff, the draggled black skull-cap with its torn binding, and the unravelled woollen remnant of braid that completed the circle.

'Cynric told simple truth, and here are the proofs of it.

Only this morning, when I saw Mistress Hammet's open hand once again, and remembered the grazes I had dressed, did I understand how she got those injuries. Not from a fall – there was no fall. The wound on her head was dealt by this staff, for I found several long hairs of her greying light-brown colour here, caught in the frayed edges of this silver band. You see it's worn wafer-thin, and the edges turned and cracking.'

Radulfus ran a long, lean finger round the crumpled, razor-sharp rim, and nodded grimly. 'Yes, I see. And from this same band she got the grazes to her hands. He swung his staff at her a second time, so Cynric said, and she caught and clung to it, to save her head. . . .'

'. . . and he tugged at it with all his strength, and tore it by main force out of her hands,' said Hugh, 'to his own undoing.'

'They could not have been many paces past the mill,' said Cadfael, 'for Cynric was some way beyond, among the willows. On the side of that first stump that overhangs the pool I found a few broken withies, and this black ravelling of wool braid snagged in the cracked, dead wood of the stump. The priest went stunned or dazed into the water, the cap flew from his head, leaving this scrap held fast in the tree, as the silver band held her torn hairs. The staff was flung from his hand. The winter turf is tufted and rough there, no wonder if he caught his heel, as he reeled backwards when she loosed her hold. He crashed into the stump. The axe that felled it, long ago, left it uneven, the jagged edge took him low at the back of the head. Father, you saw the wound. So did the sheriff.'

'I saw it,' said Radulfus. 'And the woman knew nothing from the time she ran from him?'

'She barely knows how she got home. Certainly she waited out the night in dread, expecting him to finish what he intended against the boy, and return to his house to denounce and cast her out. But he never came.'

'Could he have been saved?' wondered the abbot, grieving

as much for the roused and resentful flock as for the dead shepherd.

'In the dark,' said Cadfael, 'I doubt if any one man could have got him from under that bank, however he laboured at it. Even had there been help within reach, I think he would have drowned before ever they got him out.'

'At the risk of falling into sin,' said Radulfus, with a smile that began sourly and ended in resignation, 'I find that comforting. We have not a murderer among us, at any rate.'

'Talk of falling into sin,' said Cadfael later, when he and Hugh were sitting easy together in the workshop in the herb garden, 'forces me to examine my own conscience. I enjoy some privileges, by reason of being called on to attend sick people outside the enclave, and also by virtue of having a godson to visit. But I ought not to take advantage of that permission for my own ends. Which I have done shamelessly on three or four occasions since Christmas. Indeed, Father Abbot must be well aware that I went out from the precinct this very morning without leave, but he's said no word about it.'

'No doubt he takes it for granted you'll be making proper confession voluntarily, at chapter tomorrow,' said Hugh, straight-faced.

'That I doubt! He'd hardly welcome it. I should have to explain the reason, and I know his mind by now. There are old hawks like Radulfus and myself in here, who can stand the gales, but there are also innocents who will not benefit by too stormy a wind blowing through the dovecote. He's fretted enough about Ailnoth's influence, now he wants it put by and soon forgotten. And I prophesy, Hugh, that the Foregate will soon have a new priest, and one who is known and welcome not only to us who have the bestowing of the benefice, but to those who are likely to reap the results. No better way of burying Ailnoth.'

'In all fairness,' said Hugh thoughtfully, 'it would have been a very delicate matter to reject a priest recommended by the papal legate, even for a man of your abbot's stature. And the fellow was impressive to the eye and the ear, and had scholarship. . . . No wonder Radulfus thought he was bringing you a treasure. God send you a decent, humble, common man next time.'

'Amen! Whether he has Latin or not! And here am I the well-wisher, if not the accomplice, of an enemy of the King, criminal as well as sinner! Did I say I was being obliged to search my conscience? But not too diligently – that always leads to trouble.'

'I wonder,' said Hugh, smiling indulgently into the glow of the brazier, 'if they'll have set out yet?'

'Not until dark, I fancy. Overnight they'll be gone. I hope she has somehow left word for Ralph Giffard,' said Cadfael, considering. 'He's no bad man, only driven, as so many are now, and mainly for his son. She had no complaint of him, except that he had compounded with fortune, and given up his hopes for the Empress. Being more than thirty years short of his age, she finds that incomprehensible. But you and I, Hugh, can comprehend it all too well. Let the young ones go their own gait, and find their own way.'

He sat smiling, thinking of the pair of them, but chiefly of Ninian, lively and bold and impudent, and a stout performer with the spade, even though he had never had one in his hand before, and had to learn the craft quickly. 'I never had such a stout-hearted labourer under me here since Brother John – that must be nearly five years now! The one who stayed in Gwytherin, and married the smith's niece. He'll have made a doughty smith himself by now. Benet reminded me of him, some ways . . . all or nothing, and ready for every venture.'

'Ninian,' said Hugh, correcting him almost absently.

'True, Ninian we must call him now, but I tend to forget. But I haven't told you,' said Cadfael, kindling joyfully to the recollection, 'the very best of the ending. In the middle of so much aggravation and suspicion and death, a joke is no bad thing.'

'I wouldn't say no to that,' agreed Hugh, leaning forward

to mend the fire with a few judiciously placed pieces of charcoal, with the calculated pleasure of one for whom such things are usually done by others. 'But I saw very little sign of one today. Where did you find it?'

'Why, you were kept busy talking with Father Abbot, close by the grave, while the rest were dispersing. You had no chance to observe it. But I was loose, and so was Brother Jerome, with his nose twitching for officious mischief, as usual. Sanan saw it,' said Cadfael, with fond recollection. 'It scared the wits out of her for a moment or two, but then it was all resolved. You know, Hugh, how wide those double doors of ours are, in the wall. . . .'

'I came that way,' said Hugh patiently, a little sleepy with relief from care, the fumes of the brazier, and the early start to a day now subsiding into a dim and misty evening. 'I know!'

'There was a young fellow holding a horse, out there in the Foregate. Who was to notice him until everyone began streaming out by that way? Jerome was running like a sheep-dog about the fringes, hustling them out, he was bound to take a frequent look out there to the streets. He saw a man he thought he recognised, and went closer to view, all panting with fervour and zeal – you know him!'

'Every uncoverer of evil acquires merit,' said Hugh, taking idle pleasure in the mild satire upon Brother Jerome. 'What merit could there be for him there, in a lad holding a horse?'

'Why, one Benet, or Ninian, hunted as recreant to our lord King Stephen, and denounced to our lord sheriff – saving your presence, Hugh, but you know you were just confirmed in office, you mean more now to Brother Jerome than ever before! – by Ralph Giffard, no less. That is what Jerome saw, barring that the malefactor did seem to be wearing clothes never seen on him before.'

'Now you do surprise me,' said Hugh, turning a gleaming and amused face upon his friend. 'And this really was the said Benet or Ninian?'

'It was indeed. I knew him, and so did Sanan when she

looked ahead, where Jerome was looking, and saw him there. The lad himself, Hugh, bold as ever to plunge his head into whatever snare. Come to make sure himself where the blame was flying, and see that none of it fell upon his nurse. God knows what he would have done, if you had not carolled aloud your preference for Jordan. After all, what did he know of all that happened after he came panting into the church, that night? It could have been Jordan, for all he knew. No doubt he believed it was, once you bayed the quarry.'

'I have a fine, bell-mouthed bay,' acknowledged Hugh, grinning. 'And just as well Father Abbot kept me talking and would have me stay and dine with him, or I might have run my nose full into this madcap lad of yours, and just as Jerome plucked him by the hood. So how did all this end? I heard no foray in the Foregate.'

'There was none,' agreed Cadfael complacently. 'Ralph Giffard was there among the crowd, did you never see him? He's tall enough to top most of the Foregate folk. But there, you were held fast in the middle, no time to look about you. He was there. At the end he turned to go, not worst pleased, I fancy, that you had no hold on the lad he'd felt obliged to hand to you earlier. It was good to see, Hugh! He shouldered past Jerome, having legs so much longer, just as our most eager hound had his nose down on a hot scent. And he took the bridle from the lad's hand, and even smiled at him, eye to eye, and the lad held his stirrup for him and steadied him astride, as good a groom as ever you saw. And Jerome baulked like a hound at a loss, and came scuttling back, aghast that he'd as good as howled accusation at Giffard's own groom, waiting honestly for his master. That was when I saw Sanan shudder into such laughter as might almost have broken her apart, but that she's very sturdily made, that lady! And Giffard rode away, back along the Foregate, and the groom that was no groom of his went trotting after him afoot, out of sight and away.'

'And this verily happened?' demanded Hugh.

'Son, I saw it. I shall cherish it. Off they went, and Ralph Giffard threw a silver penny to young Ninian, and Ninian caught it and went on his way round the corner and out of sight, before he stopped for breath. And still does not know, I suppose,' said Cadfael, peering through the doorway into a late afternoon light that still lacked an hour or so to Vespers, 'still does not know to whom he owes his salvation. How I would love to be by, when Sanan tells him to whom he owes his fat pay for less than an hour of holding a horse! I wager that lad will never part with that penny, he'll have it pierced for his neck or for hers. There are not many such keepsakes,' said Cadfael smugly, 'in one lifetime.'

'Are you telling me,' said Hugh, delighted, 'that those two met so and parted so, in mutual service, and had no notion with whom they dealt?'

'No notion in the world! They had exchanged messages, they were allies, adversaries, friends, enemies, what you please, in the most intimate degree,' said Cadfael, with deep and grateful contentment, 'but neither of them had the least idea what the other one looked like. They had never once set eyes on each other.'